W9-CPP-937

Also by Bernard Cooper

Truth Serum
A Year of Rhymes
Maps to Anywhere

guess again

short stories

Bernard Cooper

SIMON & SCHUSTER
New York London Toronto
Sydney Singapore

SIMON & SCHUSTER
Rockefeller Center
1230 Avenue of the Americas
New York, NY 10020

SIMON & SCHUSTER and colophon are registered trademarks of Simon & Schuster, Inc.

Designed by Kyoko Watanabe

Manufactured in the United States of America

10 9 8 7 6 5 4 3 2 1

Library of Congress Cataloging-in-Publication Data

Cooper, Bernard, date.
    Guess Again / Bernard Cooper.
        p. cm.
        Contents: Night sky—Intro to Acting—What to name the baby—X—Bit-O-Honey—Hunters and gatherers—A man in the making—Exterior decoration—Graphology—Between the sheets—Old birds.
        1. United States—Social life and customs—20th century—Fiction. I. Title.
    PS3553.O5798 G84 2000
    813'.54—dc21   00-041293
    ISBN 0-684-86586-6

Some of these stories appeared, sometimes in different form, in the following publications:

"Exterior Decoration" in *The LA Weekly*; "X" in *The Mid-American Review*; "Between the Sheets" in *Nerve*; "Intro to Acting" in *The North American Review*; "Old Birds" in *The Paris Review*; "Hunters and Gatherers" in *Ploughshares*; "What to Name the Baby" and "Night Sky" in *Story*; and "Bit-O-Honey" in *The Threepenny Review*.

Acknowledgments

The author wishes to thank the John Simon Guggenheim Foundation and the John Paul Getty Center for the Arts and Humanities for their generous support while many of these stories were written.

Thanks, also, to the following individuals for their insight and kindness: Will Allison, Hilton Als, Steven Barclay, Kimberly Burns, Jill Ciment, Mark Doty, Peter Gadol, Amy Gerstler, Jeff Hammond, Sloan Harris, Eloise Klein Healy, Michelle Huneven, Geoff Kloske, Tom Knechtel, Bia Lowe, Michael Lowenthal, Lisa Michaels, Brian Miller, Beaty Reynolds, Greg Riley, Aleida Rodríguez, Lois Rosenthal, Michael Sledge, and Benjamin Weissman.

Contents

Some say that love's a little boy,
And some say it's a bird,
Some say it makes the world go round,
And some say that's absurd,
And when I asked the man next-door,
Who looked as if he knew,
His wife got very cross indeed,
And said it wouldn't do.
Does it look like a pair of pyjamas,
Or a ham in a temperance hotel?
Does its odour remind one of llamas,
Or has it a comforting smell?
Is it prickly to touch as a hedge is,
Or soft as eiderdown fluff?
Is it sharp or quite smooth at the edges?
O tell me the truth about love.

—W. H. AUDEN

guess again

night sky

As Kay shouted instructions in the background, I angled the telescope down the mountain toward the home of her ex-husband, but no matter how carefully I focused the lens or adjusted the tripod, I couldn't make out much more than a tile roof surrounded by trees. Each time I blinked, my eyelashes splayed against the glass.

"It's the wall to the left of the front door," she yelled. "Just below his driveway. See any damage?"

What little I could see of Warren's house looked fine to me, no gaping hole or trace of rubble. When I turned around and shrugged at Kay, she shrugged, too. She stood above me on the patio, lit by the blaze of an orange afternoon, her bathrobe flapping. The fierce wind blew her hair to one side, where it whipped from her head like a wind sock. The patio was as far as she could stray from the house before her electronic ankle bracelet set off an alarm at the Bel Air Police Department. Whenever this happened, a concerned officer phoned within a minute and interrogated whoever answered in order to verify Kay's whereabouts. Even if she answered the phone herself, which was usually the case, they had a way of quizzing her to make sure the voice didn't belong to some kind of Kay impersonator.

According to Kay, the main problem with house arrest was the fact that her swimming pool, embedded in a flagstone terrace several steps below the patio, was now off-limits. She loved nothing more than drifting on an inflatable raft and dangling her hands in the tepid water, a mindless hydrotherapy that helped her forget a vindictive divorce. Now that she couldn't bob across it, the water flaunted its soothing blue. The only thing that made exile from her own swimming pool tolerable was Kay's fear that the ankle bracelet would electrocute her if she dove in, even though Our Lady of Corrections, as she called her probation officer, assured her the device was waterproof. Still, Kay swore she dangled one leg outside the tub when she took a bath, largely, it seemed to me, to add yet another inconvenience to an already long list—all, she claimed, because Warren had the gall to report her.

The telescope stood on a small promontory just beyond the pool, a vantage point from which, on a day as windy as this, the city beneath us stretched in unexpected directions, the world more vivid and unfamiliar than it had been for several smoggy months. Skyscrapers jutted from downtown on one end of the horizon, and Century City on the other. A silver ribbon of sea glittered in the distance. I worked a crimp from my lower back and promised Kay I'd spy again later.

"'Investigate,'" she corrected.

I climbed back toward the patio. "You'd be a lot better off if you learned to control your temper."

She shot me the look of stunned betrayal she usually reserved for Warren. "Don't tell me *you* don't believe me, either?" Kay settled onto a chaise longue, tapped a cigarette from the pack, and tried unsuccessfully to light it against the wind. Only when I bent to cup the flame did she realize the steps had left me out of breath. She patted the chaise.

"I believe you," I said, squeezing beside her, "but I also believe some accidents happen on purpose."

"It was a strange car, Sam, a make I've never driven before."

"Every car has an emergency brake. To keep the thing from rolling downhill."

"I put it in Park!" She flicked an ash into the wind. "I'm almost certain."

When my laughter turned into hacking, I had to sit upright. Each cough felt like pumice in my lungs. Lights exploded when I closed my eyes. Kay stubbed out her cigarette and pounded me between the shoulder blades, firm the way I liked it, until the coughing stopped.

"All right," she conceded. "Maybe it was subconscious . . ."

"*Un*conscious."

"Don't correct me when I'm venting!" She cinched her robe, then tied the belt in a big angry bow. "Maybe it was *un*conscious. But I don't care about that bastard enough to back a rental car into his living room. Besides, I wouldn't have had to rent the car in the first place if he hadn't completely cleaned me out." She threw an arm behind her head, pointing in the general direction of her huge French Regency house, now vacant except for a box spring and mattress, a television set propped on a stack of phone books, and a checkered picnic blanket where the dining room table used to seat fourteen. I lay back beside her, and we listened to shuddering palm fronds and the distant clatter of what must have been a trash bin over-turning. If you let yourself, it was easy to imagine the Santa Ana turning doorknobs and peeling paint. After a while, Kay raised a lotion-polished leg—I used to love to run my cheek along those legs—and gazed at the contraption strapped to her ankle. "It's really no different from a ball and chain," she said, pointing her toes and flexing her foot to emphasize the shapely calf.

"Or one of those tracking devices they attach to wild animals."

Kay turned to face me, and touched my arm. In the ten years I'd known her, I'd never been able to second-guess what little remark would make her grateful.

When I awoke, I saw that Kay still lay beside me, nursing a tumbler of scotch. The sun was dousing itself inch by inch in the Pacific, the dying light reflected in her Ray-Bans. She gazed toward the sunset in steely contemplation, like someone pre-pared for the next grim surprise. When I first met Kay she'd been a student, the kind of young woman who pronounced "chaise longue" with a sarcastic French accent, and didn't care about the difference between cheap whiskey and single-malt scotch. But all of that changed when she married Warren. "Sam," she'd told me shortly after they met, holding my hand to buffer the blow, "Warren can give me the things I need most." I knew it was true. A successful lawyer, Warren offered Kay the constancy I couldn't, not to mention a six-figure salary and a mansion in Bel Air. And, if Warren was even half as horny as Kay implied, the guy could provide her with sex on tap. In short, Warren was a man with plenty of extras, and no one deserved them more than my wife.

Kay and I had been married—a quick civil ceremony after breakfast at Denny's—while attending graduate school at Caltech. Our Pasadena apartment, furnished with orange crates and cinder-block shelves, held the sum of our possessions, mostly books for classes on calculus, astrophysics, and a seminar devoted to the hypothesis that black holes swallowed their own light. Kay was a brilliant student, vocal in class, asking the professors challenging questions. I felt proud of Kay, safe in her presence, as though her rigorous powers of reason could protect me from harm.

Soon enough, though, Kay's scholastic daring showed its dark side. She turned in long, argumentative essays for exams she could have aced. She offered a group of physics majors the unsolicited opinion that their model of cold fusion, with its Styrofoam balls and plastic tubing, looked like a kid's project for a science fair. She filed her nails during peer reviews. All this happened in the second year of our marriage, and I couldn't help but see myself as the cause. Kay's brazenness existed in direct proportion to my secrecy. The more I suppressed my desire for men, the more keenly Kay seemed to sense its strength. Even if this conviction—that the changes in her behavior hinged on my inner life—arose from youthful egotism, her alertness to my moods was real, and precisely the trait that made leaving her so difficult.

Then along came Warren Scofield for a graduate lecture on scientific patents. Kay returned from his lecture all hopped up about the ethical and legal ramifications of a bioengineered bacterium that was supposed to eat oil spills, though no one was certain what else it might feast on when thrown in the ocean. She paced back and forth and recounted the lecture point by point, calling Warren by his first name once too often. I knew right then they would sleep together, and this freed me to flirt with the handsome guy in Financial Aid who filed my paperwork. After the split, Kay and I were amazed at how quickly we shifted into friendship—though we still can't talk about those old infidelities without a fight—as if divorce had been the prelude to a far more doable union.

That night on her patio, moments from our marriage reached me like starlight, their origins a long way off. I lay there as Kay sipped liquor, wind ruffling the collar of her robe. She chewed an ice cube, huffing at thoughts, I supposed, of Warren. While I'd slept, she'd covered me with a blanket, and now the idea of trying to untangle myself was exhausting. Those were the days before protease inhibitors, when I thought the virus was going to destroy me sooner rather than later, and sleep was the only antidote to my fearful, finite point of view: last visit with Kay; last windy night; last glance through a telescope—the litany would begin the instant I opened my eyes. When Kay felt me stirring she reached over and, without shifting her gaze from the view, yanked at the blanket, setting me free. I yawned and stretched, clenched the feeling back into my fingers. While I waited for wakefulness to take hold, the avenues below us ignited with lights. Underneath a darkening sky, the city looked sad and dazzling, like a picture postcard someone never sent.

And then I saw, or thought I saw, a surge of light. An electrical charge was sucked from the air, leaving an indescribable void as every refrigerator, power tool, garage door opener, and chandelier in the neighborhood went dead. Houses all around us were suddenly extinguished. A new moon, still low in the east, cast a faint glow.

"Say it's not me," said Kay. She grabbed my hand—we both winced at a shock of static—and peered into her dark yard. Lit from within only seconds ago, the swimming pool had disappeared. Wind stripped the leaves from trees, the air alive with grit and friction. Below us, the only lights left in the city belonged to traffic that had no doubt come to a halt at dim intersections. In the vicinity of West Hollywood, a hospital with its own generator twinkled like a sequin on a bolt of black fabric.

Kay's shadowy figure rose from the chaise, ice cubes clinking. "I'm making a break," she said, gulping the dregs of her scotch.

"What?"

"I'm returning to the scene of the crime. Bet the damage isn't half as bad as he claimed in the police report."

"You're not going to Warren's."

"Why not?

"You're under house arrest, remember?"

"Oh, honey. You're too good for your own . . . good."

"What'll I tell Our Lady?"

Kay raised her leg and dangled her ankle. "I'm sure this thing won't work during a blackout."

"It runs on batteries, Kay. And the phones work during a power outage."

She stepped into a pair of sandals. "What I'm saying is, the precinct will be swamped with calls, and no one's going to go chasing after a first offender. Or nouveau offender, as they say in these parts." Before I could stop her, she dashed inside the house. I followed the scent of Bain de Soleil. It was a good thing Warren had taken all the furniture, because the place was pitch dark, and I would have caused a fortune in damage or broken my neck. In her white robe, Kay made a spectral exit out the front door. "Stay here, Sam," she called over her shoulder. "I'll be back in no time."

The phone began to ring. "See, Kay?" I shouted, but she kept on padding down the street.

I didn't relish the idea of having to talk to Kay's probation officer; in previous conversations, she'd been far too canny to fall for a lie. Still, I ran to get it because I hate the ring of an unanswered phone—a sound close to hopeless. I plucked the phone off the living room floor. "Hi," I panted. "Kay's indisposed . . ."

"This is an important message from the Brokerage Firm of Hansen and Wong. Are you one of the thousands of Americans who's put off preparing for retirement?" I would have hung up—the message, after all, was prerecorded—but I needed a moment to catch my breath. "Whether you're looking for the security of low-risk bonds or the adventure of high-growth stocks, it's never too late to invest in the future." The male voice was without inflection, like a robot's admonishment. It gave the night a futuristic tinge. I stood in the empty living room, with its panoramic view of the missing city, and wondered why I'd studied science.

It was foolish to try and catch up with Kay. Even if my lungs could get me downhill, there was uphill to contend with. But anything was better than being alone in Kay's empty house, waiting for the phone to echo through its rooms.

I set off from the front porch with an unusual burst of energy, but soon found that the best way to make progress was to take small, methodical steps. It was one thing for me to walk haltingly at my supermarket in West Hollywood, where the shoppers had seen so many failing bodies that no one gawked at the sight of lesions, Hickman catheters, or gaunt young men shuffling down the aisles. But a lone man lurching down Copa de Oro was another matter, especially since there aren't any sidewalks in Bel Air and the residents tend to panic at the sight of foot traffic. Several houses had motion detectors bolted to their fences and stone walls; anyone so much as sneezing within a thirty-foot radius would set off a floodlight worthy of San Quentin. But now, of course, none of them worked, the gloom a kind of protective cloak. Without electricity, perhaps the rules of etiquette relaxed. Even Kay's wandering about the neighborhood in her bathrobe might strike the ordinarily wary onlooker as a neighbor's endearing response to the crisis. *Under cover of darkness,* I said to myself, forging ahead.

Each house I passed—at least the ones I could see behind high walls and extravagant foliage—was another brand of fantasy: rustic Tudor, low-slung ranch, boxy modern. Here and there, windows flickered with the beams of flashlights or the mild, floating corona of candles. In one house I heard the cries of children, lost it seemed in a labyrinth of rooms. I passed enormous monogrammed gates, a birdbath shaped like a giant champagne glass, and a formerly Negroid lawn jockey who hoisted a plaster lantern, his face repainted to look Caucasian. Under a tunnel of jacaranda, I tramped through a blizzard of lavender petals, the hot wind ballooning inside my shirt.

Once I'd been a jogger. Sure of my body. I used to lift my lover off his feet and make him yelp like a gleeful child, and even later, when he grew too weak to walk on his own, I carried him to and from the bed. Now every exertion, every gesture, no matter how brief or easy or routine, exacted a price.

When I turned the corner onto Bellagio, I spotted Kay sitting on the manicured lawn across the street from Warren's. The night was sweltering, but she hugged her knees as though she were cold. I buckled beside her and tried to speak, a wheeze at the crest of every breath.

"You sound awful," she said. "I told you not to follow me."

"He's not worth it, Kay. He wants some demure little flower for a wife."

"A woman who knows when to set her emergency brake."

"Exactly. Besides, you'll get a huge chunk of money when you sell the house."

Kay sighed. "And live the life to which I've grown accustomed." She rubbed her skin where the ankle bracelet chafed.

"I hate to say it, Kay, but I wouldn't mind having problems like yours."

"I know," she said, turning to face me. Even in the dark, I could see her moist, red-rimmed eyes. "Why do you think I go on and on about Warren when you're around? I hate hearing myself, but I'm afraid if I stop, there's only one topic. Your health, I mean. Your T-cells dropping. It scares me to death. And there's nothing I can do." Dogs around us began to bark at some disruption only they could hear.

Save me, I wanted to say. Ever since my diagnosis I'd said it silently, again and again, to no one in particular. I heard the words in my head like a pulse, blurted them to strangers in dreams. And there I was, fighting the urge to say it to Kay, a plea so unequivocal and blunt, resisting it took the rest of my strength.

I lay back on the grass and, gazing overhead, saw a swath of night sky. Stars congested the deep regions of space, a spectacle I'd missed while watching my steps on the leaf-strewn roads. "Kay," I said, tugging her down. Hard-pressed to take her eyes off Warren's house, she lowered her head slowly, long hair coiling beneath her like rope. Kay ran her hands through the brittle grass and her robe fell open, revealing the yellow bikini underneath. I pointed at the sky. "It's like floating on a raft."

"It is," she whispered. Some people might have searched for constellations—Ram, Hunter, Charioteer—but Kay bristled when earthly forms were imposed on the cosmos, which we'd dubbed in school the Big Abstraction. The two of us squinted at a quadrant of sky where Kay had once located the misty hint of a nebula through her telescope. Its cosmic debris and clouds of dust sailed outward at fantastic speeds, though the nebula would look, from this vast a distance, completely still for the next billion years. In a few minutes, the power around us would sputter back to life, and we'd sit up and see, through a hole Kay had made in the house across the street, Warren peering toward us, just as a patrol car screeched around the curve. But for now we lay back on a stranger's lawn, pointing to what we guessed were red dwarfs, stars formed long before the earth, their matter decaying so slowly it defies all measure of time.

intro to acting

The bouncer, a big bald slab of a man, gave Walter the once-over, then raised his hand to block the way. "Hold it," he said. Perched atop a stool outside the bar's entrance, massive shoulders protruding from a tank top, he was taller than Walter even when seated. His palm pressed against Walter's chest, and a welcome human heat seeped through Walter's tie and dress shirt, causing him pleasure as well as surprise—he hadn't been touched by a man in months. "Our dress code is strictly enforced," announced the bouncer. A deep vibrato traveled down his arm and rattled Walter's ribs.

"You brute," said a man standing behind Walter. A line was beginning to form. "Give the boy a break or I'll tell him your nickname."

This threat caused the bouncer to blush panoramically. "I don't make the rules," he said.

"He makes needlepoint pillows," said the man, who Walter figured was a regular. "That's why we call him Granny Sampler."

"You bitch," growled the bouncer, but the hint of a grin flickered on his lips.

"So?" asked Walter. "You letting me in?" For weeks now, after late nights in the Paramount conference room, when fatigue and eyestrain and the tightening vise of a headache made him too weary to resist, Walter would drive past the Hammer on his way home. Rows of motorcycles gleamed in the sulfurous light of its parking lot. Some nights he'd catch a glimpse of leather-clad patrons strutting toward the door, an occasional shirtless back among them, or a bare ass, pale as a cameo, framed in black chaps. Walter pictured the place crowded with guys in provocative poses. Mankind on a platter.

But now there was some commotion over the clothes he hadn't changed after work, the bouncer fingering the lapel of Walter's jacket as though he were deciding whether to buy it. "This isn't leather," he said to Walter's advocate, "it's suede."

"A technicality," said the man.

"Civilization is made of technicalities," countered the bouncer.

"And what," asked the man, "does civilization have to do with this establishment? Now loosen your sphincter and let the kid in."

Walter found it strangely satisfying to be talked about without having to respond. It was the opposite of what he'd done that day at work—pitch movie ideas to studio heads who were petrified into a state of boredom from which no plot synopsis, however dense with sex or explosions, could possibly rouse them.

"Can we get this line moving?" someone shouted.

"What's the problem?" asked the bouncer. "You turn into a pumpkin after midnight?"

"Yes," said the culprit, stepping outside the line in order to identify himself. "Yes, I do." A ring pierced his lower lip and this made him look perhaps more petulant than he actually was. He wore matching studded armbands that gripped his flesh as tightly as tourniquets. Here and there his body was bisected with tattoos of barbed wire, and Walter, who'd spun around to see how long the line had become, got the impression that the man, desperate for a night on the town, had hastily assembled himself from spare parts.

The line was still relatively short, though it was clear that, without exception, each of the Hammer's patrons was dressed in at least one item of black leather, and this qualified everyone but Walter for membership in the Brotherhood of the Hide. Driving by the bar that night, Walter had decided it was now or never and swerved his BMW into the first available parking space. Leaping from the car, eager to finally step over the Hammer's threshold, he hadn't realized until too late just how conspicuous he would be. He began to perspire and removed his jacket, which Granny Sampler grabbed out of his hand and, after a glance at the satin lining, held aloft for everyone to see. "Suede," he barked. "Says so on the label."

A collective groan arose from the lengthening line, nearly drowning out the techno music whose sinister rhythm pulsed from the entrance. Just then a mustachioed man in a California Highway Patrol uniform, minus the badge that could get him arrested for impersonating an officer, parted the leather fringe covering the doorway. "Suede *is* leather," he announced, having caught the last snatch of controversy. He planted a kiss on the bouncer's glossy head, then swaggered toward the parking lot. Walter thought this might settle the matter, but the bouncer told him to ditch the jacket or come back another night.

"Is there a coatroom?" asked Walter.

"He wants to know if there's a coatroom," bellowed the bouncer. Several people snickered. A muscular couple, either twins or lovers, bailed out of line and headed home. "Sure, guy, the maître d' will show you where it is."

"Will somebody please get Phil?" demanded the man with the lip ring. "The doorman's drunk with power!"

"I'm corrupted absolutely," said the bouncer. "Tell you what," he proposed to the men in line. "I'll talk to Phil, and if he says this is leather, you're all in, no cover. But if he says it's not, Barbie Wire down there is going to pay for each and every one of you."

"Fine by me," said the man with the lip ring. "Just move it, will ya? I'm not spending Saturday night standing in line because some Einstein doesn't know that leather and suede are the same animal."

The bouncer slid from his perch, parted the fringe, and disappeared, leaving a jacketless Walter standing before the entryway, his white shirt bright as a klieg light. He stepped away from the stool so none of the new arrivals would know that he was the overdressed obstacle who'd caused the night to grind to a halt. The man who'd been standing in line behind him, so hirsute he appeared to be wearing a sweater beneath his leather vest, tried to comfort Walter by assuring him that this, or some hassle like it, happened all the time. "Just imagine you're in New Guinea," he said, "and this is some primitive rite of passage."

Walter wiped the sweat from his forehead. "That about sums it up," he said.

Lou introduced himself, said he was a professor of anthropology at UCLA, and asked Walter what he did. "For a living," Lou added, since asking someone what he "did" might be easily misconstrued at the Hammer. Walter told Lou about working at Paramount. While he and Lou talked, Walter thrust his hands into the Di-Gels and lint at the bottom of his pockets. He could feel the folded crib notes he'd used in tonight's meeting, a story idea by the writer Rodney Culp, whose latest hit involved a beloved but deranged baseball player who, after being traded to another team, dumps a vial of anthrax into the concession stand at Shea Stadium. *Doomsday Playoffs* had kept the studio in the black during a season of what Al Neiman, president of development, called "art-house money-shredders," most of which had been ushered into production by none other than Walter himself. And tonight he'd had a chance to redeem himself with Culp's latest project, a three-paragraph treatment about a Neanderthal man whose slapstick courtship of a voluptuous cavewoman causes rock slides and brushfires and, through a series of geological events Walter found difficult to explain, the eruption of a once-dormant volcano. The dinosaurs become extinct at the end of ninety minutes, though the couple survives to mate amid the devastation, insuring the continuation of the human race.

"Funny premise," Neiman had said, "but there's lots of apocalypse." Walter couldn't tell if this was a compliment or a criticism, and Neiman's shiny unlined face, recently lifted, didn't yield a clue. Others present at the pitch were also stymied by Neiman's response, and no one dared venture a word of either agreement or dissent. Everyone turned to Walter. Janet Schiff, a former reader and now the only woman on salary, looked especially beseeching, since she more than anyone was afraid to say the wrong thing.

"Names are attached to this project," blurted Walter. "Big names."

"Are we talking Tom Cruise?" asked Neiman, "Or one of those prissy bum-fucks from Merrie Olde England?"

Walter saw Janet bristle in the periphery of his vision. "It's Schwarzenegger," he lied, praying he could contact the actor's agent first thing tomorrow.

"What's the outlook on product tie-ins?" asked Bert Halverstrom from Marketing.

"How about lava soft drinks?" suggested Janet.

"Too much like the Swamp Water we did for *Lost Lagoon*," said Neiman. "We'll have to work on a Stone Age collectible." He tapped his manicured fingers on the table. "What about the rating? If there's screwing at the end, can we make it arty enough to get a PG?"

"Schwarzenegger doesn't do nude," said Marty Scarwood, "so it's not a problem."

"The talent these days," Neiman lamented, shaking his head. "The man's tuchis is hanging out of a loincloth in *Conan*, but he won't do nude."

"About Culp's people," said Walter.

"Schnapps!" shouted Neiman.

"Pardon?"

"Break out the peppermint schnapps," he said, rolling his chair away from the table and barreling toward the built-in bar. "Tell Culp's people his project's got legs."

Walter's breath was still candied from the peppermint schnapps he and Janet had tossed back, a sweet anesthesia, while sharing looks that said they'd have a lot to talk about later. "How I envy you kids," Neiman had told them, nursing the contents of his shot glass. "You can drink quarts of this panty remover and still be fresh for work in the morning."

Walter was counting on something stronger than schnapps if and when the bouncer let him in. At this rate, he might be too tired and hung-over to show up at work the next day. He didn't have to call Schwarzenegger's agent, tomorrow or ever. He could always lie and say the actor wasn't interested, or expected a preposterous share of the profits. Neiman loved to rant about celebrities anyway; they were pampered, demanding, vain as peacocks, and he never tired of mocking the amenities written into their contracts: an on-location astrologer, oranges flown in from Florida. "What's next?" he once grumbled. "A Nubian masseuse?" Neiman would probably enjoy fuming more than he would signing a honey of a deal, so Walter, really, would be doing him a favor.

Ever since becoming a producer at Paramount, Walter hadn't had a day to himself. Twenty-four hours without last-minute script revisions or consultations with the studio lawyers, a cell phone practically grafted to his ear, was as hard for him to grasp as higher mathematics. He could barely remember what it was like to eat lunch alone, and prided himself on being able to talk business and chew food at the same time, no stray particles flying from his mouth or clinging to his teeth. Once, he knew enthusiasm for a great screenplay in the pit of his stomach, but now every day was filled with the hype and reflexive white lies—"This is a hot property"; "You'll hear from us next week"—he relied on to spare a writer's feelings, get cozy with a powerful agent, or end a tedious meeting early.

Praise was little more than a convenience, and his opinions eventually circled back as dubious rumor.

Walter glanced at his watch—the bouncer had been gone for what seemed like a long time—and the late hour clinched it: He'd call in sick. But when he tried to imagine the following day, it was vast and white, forlorn as an ice floe. Even when he was a boy, solitude made Walter anxious, a bad break for an only child. Left alone in his room, he'd wallow in a jumble of blocks and hand puppets and plastic cars, dazed by the infinite options of play. Walter felt safer being told what to do.

More and more these days, between power lunches and conference calls, Walter fantasized that a sexy, temperamental man was giving him orders. Walter's task—equal parts joy and unthinking obedience—was to paint the man's body, muscle by muscle, limb by limb, with strokes of his tongue. Each time this fantasy occurred, Walter felt like Michelangelo suspended on a scaffold at the Sistine Chapel—flat on his back, all rapturous effort, gazing up at a burly God.

"You might try rolling up your sleeves," suggested Lou, "and—not that you asked—but if I were you, I'd pop open a couple of buttons and show some skin." Lou's fuss made Walter grateful, if a little embarrassed that his need to get laid was so obvious it inspired advice from a total stranger. They stood face to face, and Walter wondered what it would be like to rest his head against Lou's hairy chest; but as sometimes happened at bars like the Hammer, brotherly roles could be set in stone the moment two men met. Walter folded his tie and slipped it into his back pocket. After he'd rearranged his outfit, he was able to relax a little, though the shirt was still starched and out of place, and no amount of Lou's sartorial origami would change that.

Lou nudged Walter and nodded toward the bouncer's stool. Squashed atop it lay a needlepoint pillow of a hammer, the head done in metallic yarn—Granny's handiwork. "Someday," said Lou, "we'll be studying artifacts like that along with amphorae and fertility statues."

And Stone Age collectibles, thought Walter.

The bouncer burst through the doorway. He tossed the jacket and Walter caught it. "Gentlemen," said a chastened Granny Sampler. "No stampeding, please." He winked at Walter and drew the leather fringe aside.

Jacket draped over one arm, Walter stepped into a bar that was far darker and more claustrophobic than any he'd been to in West Hollywood. He had to squeeze through a gauntlet of men whose eyes appraised him then darted away. The few who bothered to look at him with any interest were merely taking note, Walter was certain, of his dressy shirt, and in defiance of the drudge he'd become, he unbuttoned it all the way. He regretted not having time to go to a gym, but at least meetings with Al Neiman kept him perpetually nervous and thin. Lou appeared at his side and gave his gaping shirt the thumbs-up. "I see you put your goods in the window," he said, then turned to greet a man with a Mohawk. It was hot and stuffy in the main room. Walter smelled the yeasty reek of beer and a faint odor of male sweat that reminded him of bouillon cubes. Even with his shirt hanging open, he felt modest next to men in latex shorts, or strategically ripped T-shirts, or leather harnesses framing chests whose nipples were tauntingly prominent.

The men near the door cruised with impunity, while those huddled in the dim reaches of the Hammer seemed uninterested in conversation, not to mention oxygen or light. He wedged himself between two body builders, their latissimus dorsi like swinging doors, and ordered a bourbon on the rocks. The bartender, an adorable show-off with a brush cut, lifted the bottle high above the glass and poured a strand of amber booze. Walter spotted Lou at the other end of the bar; he seemed completely at ease, buying a Perrier for the man with the Mohawk, the two of them shouting to each other over the din and throwing back their heads with laughter.

When Walter turned around with his drink, he found himself facing a row of men lined up against the wall only a few feet away. Some of them eyed the passersby, while others nodded and bobbed to the music. Convinced that no one would look at him, Walter nevertheless felt as if he were on display. Taut with self-consciousness, he didn't know how to hold his head, where to look, or what to do with his hands. Chugging alcohol did little to slow his heart rate, though it did help muffle it somewhat, like a clapper ringing in a padded bell.

Smoke wafted indoors from what must have been a patio, and Walter followed the fragrant trail to a gaggle of daddies gathered around a fire pit, sucking cigars, their faces lit from beneath by the flames. On the far wall, a mural depicted a postman whose thighs and biceps strained the seams of his uniform, letters spilling from his pouch as a hunky customer bent him over a mailbox, ready to make a delivery of his own, a hard-on the size of a Presto Log jutting out of his jeans. The mural gave Walter a jolt of purely incredulous pleasure, and as he walked toward it, he accidentally stumbled into the leash stretched between a master and his slave. Walter and the slave began a marathon of apology, saying "After you," "No, after you," until the master, bored with their self-abasement, yanked on the leash and commanded, "Heel."

Demanding masculine ego—wasn't it a force like nuclear

power or diesel fuel? Didn't it light cities and stimulate commerce? Walter could spot an alpha male from a mile away, saw them emit a virile glow that couldn't be mistaken for the paler shades of beta. Though he'd been tempted to confide in Janet, especially when they met in the commissary and wisecracked about their lousy sex lives, Walter told no one about this wish to be dominated by another man. He'd recently seen a couple of underground newspapers, *Power Monger* and *Manservant* for example, where "bottoms" who sought "tops" advertised themselves for sale in photographs that showed them naked, or dog-collared, or cinched in restraints. He could certainly understand the fantasies behind such ads, but acting them out to that extreme would require a commitment for which he had neither the temperament nor time. He had a life to lead, bills to pay, upkeep on a posh condo. Even if he could live in a cage, as was the case with some of the more dedicated slaves he'd read about, Walter would require, at the very least, fresh sawdust on the floor and an exercise wheel.

After ordering another bourbon from the patio bar, Walter settled into a corner and imagined being marched into the studio by a swarthy, dictatorial top whose torso glistened with oil. "Who's the gorilla?" Neiman would ask. And the gorilla would say, "His personal trainer."

Walter's gums were going numb, the once-pungent swigs of bourbon starting to taste as tame as milk. He leaned back and melded with the wall. Just as he was about to lapse into statuary, he was brought to his senses by a handsome man striding toward him. With sun-weathered skin and sandy hair, he was the kind of man Janet would have called outdoorsy, a little catch of lust in her throat. The effort to stand straighter on such short notice was futile, but Walter lifted his head and tried an inviting smile. "You're so vascular," said the sandy-haired man. "Where'd you get those amazing veins?" Unfortunately, he was addressing the guy beside Walter. The object of the compliment was tan and lanky and about as enticing, Walter thought grimly, as a strip of dried beef.

"Ordered 'em from a catalogue," replied the man, and the two let loose with flirtatious laughter.

Walter drained his glass and noticed that the patio had become packed in the last twenty minutes. A confounding array of sexual signs was encoded in bandannas and piercings and keys. Intimate physical features seemed magnified in the firelight—the creases in a neck, a scattering of moles, the scar from an inoculation—each revealed like a long-held secret. Walter chewed ice cubes and pondered the crowd. Did people get the faces they were born with, or the faces they deserved? Were these men behaving as they really were, or behaving the way they thought men were supposed to? Did anyone ever get what he desired, or was lust the proverbial dangling carrot, the body a mule who trotted behind?

By the third drink, weary of thinking, Walter threw himself into the stream of milling men and soon found himself back indoors, facing a vestibule he hadn't noticed earlier. A small crowd had gathered and he had to strain over the onlookers in order to see the barber chair elevated atop a black platform. In it sat a stocky older man wearing dog tags, an olive-drab T-shirt, and camouflage fatigues. At his feet knelt a younger, thinner man who snapped a chamois and buffed his boots. The older man stared into space as if he expected a shoeshine every day of his life, his nonchalance stirring the bootblack into a near frenzy of acquiescence. Hunkered over the boots, muscles rippling in his jaw, the bootblack produced a salvo of spit and licked the leather till it shone like tar. His tongue was agile, eyes rolling back. What would it be like, Walter wondered, to know a satisfaction so absolute that all other pleasure seemed pointless? Was the bootblack paid for his services, or did he do this voluntarily, bringing a chamois wherever he went? The bar was noisy, yet this scene took place in a bubble of reverential silence, no lewd jokes or murmurs of encouragement, though Walter heard, from far away, the thwacking paddles and clanging bells of what was either a pinball machine or the cranks and pulleys that turned the earth.

Lou tapped him on the shoulder. "How goes it?" he asked.

Walter wanted to tell him all sorts of things he couldn't possibly articulate, such as the fact that the air was charged with a tense hormonal readiness, which is a fine and terrible thing to breathe, for it makes you feel both alive and lonely. "Doin' good," he decided to say.

"About Granny Sampler," said Lou.

"What a schmuck."

"He's really not a bad guy when he's off duty. He's only working here to pay for acting classes. Besides, he likes you."

"Likes?"

"Has taken a liking to."

Walter almost dropped his drink. The bouncer made a perfect candidate for his fantasy; the second Walter saw him looming on his stool, he'd brought to mind a veritable Rolodex of associations: thug, bulldog, circus strongman, Mr. Clean. Yet he'd figured the bouncer was too surly to approach for a night of intimidation—a paradox that wasn't lost on Walter.

"And you know this how?" asked Walter.

"He says to me, 'Who's that cute guy in the white shirt? One of the Fortune Five Hundred?'"

Walter looked at Lou.

"Believe me, in Granny's parlance, that translates into a heap of interest."

"I don't know," said Walter.

"You will," said Lou, just as the bouncer waved at Walter from across the room.

A baritone voice broke in above the music. *Last call, gentlemen.* Several patrons scrambled to the bar, thrusting bills at the harried help. Slipping nimbly through the crowd, bar backs gathered empty bottles and mopped the counters with damp rags. Overhead, a row of hooded lights grew a little brighter, but a couple of watts was all it took to spoil the Hammer's ambience. The bartenders suddenly looked like people who were paid to stay awake. Puddles of booze and trails of wet footprints covered the floor. A muscular black man, flexed and majestic, leaned against a stack of beer cases, but for just about everyone else, feats of brash self-presentation that had been possible in the dim light were harder now to pull off with conviction. Some people fled alone, or with friends, or with a man they'd met only moments ago. Others continued to prowl through the room, eyes alert. "I'm off," said Lou, "but something tells me you'll do fine on your own." Walter tried to think of something to say—he wished Lou could be his chaperon for the rest of the night—but the bouncer was bounding toward him through the crowd, eager as a golden retriever. Walter and Lou exchanged a handshake. Then Lou was gone, and the music stopped, and the lights were turned up all the way, and Walter stood face-to-face with Granny.

*   *   *

Plumped on the bouncer's couch were needlepoint pillows of a drill, a hacksaw, and a crescent wrench. The bouncer sprawled among them, his thighs spread wide. Walter sat cross-legged on the floor and, somewhere between the outposts of the bouncer's knees, sipped a Fresca. Lamplight cast provocative shadows across the bouncer's clothes and accentuated the rugged topography of his head. Walter could barely look at him without swooning. "What's your name anyway?" he asked. While following the bouncer's taillights through the Silverlake hills, Walter had imagined gazing at his naked date and moaning, "Oh, Granny." In other words, a great deal, sexually speaking, depended on finding out the bouncer's real name.

"I'm Bob," said the bouncer. He told Walter that he'd recently moved to Hollywood after taking a couple of acting classes at Fresno State, the first of which he'd enrolled in only to fulfill the liberal arts requirement for a degree in veterinary medicine. "It was 'Intro to Acting,'" said Bob. "I went into class as a know-nothing kid and came out a convert."

"I know what you mean," said Walter, wistful for the days when he'd studied drama and first discovered Chekhov and Brecht.

"The livestock pens were deafening, but Cromwell Auditorium—that's where we had the class—was an empty, quiet space just waiting. The acoustics were incredible, and the lighting made you feel like you'd walked into a dream. When I stood on that stage, whatever I did or said seemed true, more meaningful and deep than life. In the right theater"—Bob sighed—"you can fart and it sounds like oratory." The teachers, thought Walter, must have cast him as a ruffian, a roustabout, a . . . bouncer. "Hey, Walter," said Bob, yawning and stretching his legs, "while you're down there, would you mind giving me a foot rub? It's been a long night and my feet are killing me."

Walter set his Fresca on the floor. He unlaced Bob's gym shoe and hoisted onto his lap a warm, damp, white-stockinged foot. "Would you mind" had been much too polite; Walter wanted Bob to be strict. "More forceful," he whispered, kneading Bob's heel.

"No," said Bob. "What you're doing now feels great. I've got fallen arches—probably from power lifting—and I can't take too much pressure. The stool at work was Phil's idea. . . ." Bob fell silent. "Oh," he said. "I get it." He blushed as only a bald man can: ubiquitous, crimson. "I'll boss you around in a minute, but first, would you mind doing the other foot? You're so good at this."

Flattery pretty much robbed the foot rub of the gruff thrill Walter was aiming for, but he *had* been given an order of sorts. He removed the other shoe and massaged the instep with his thumbs. While Bob struggled not to melt with helpless enjoyment, Walter grew dizzy with anticipation. Above the couch, a picture window looked out over the hills where dozens of houses, their windows dark, seemed to levitate in the predawn sky.

Finally the bouncer roused himself and growled, "You call this a foot rub!"

Walter shuddered. *It's happening,* he said to himself.

"Put your back into it, boy! I've had better foot rubs from . . . from . . ."

A wall clock ticked. A car alarm went off somewhere in the neighborhood. Walter was about to whimper, "Don't stop now!" But no sooner had he opened his mouth than the bouncer flung out his hand and sputtered, "Give me a minute." Bob closed his eyes and furrowed his brows. When the bouncer's eyes opened at last, he pounded the couch. The wrench and drill and hacksaw jumped. "I can't do this," he said. "You're a studio executive for God's sake! I feel like I'm on an audition. If only you hadn't told me you work at Paramount."

Back at the Hammer, Walter had hoped that mentioning his job might help in the seduction. Wasn't his position supposed to come with perks? "You're doing fine!"

Bob shook his head. "You're just being nice."

"No," said Walter, "*you're* just being nice."

"I'm lousy at improvisation," said the bouncer. "Antoinette, my acting coach, reminds me all the time. 'You are so . . . how can I say it, Robert, without giving to you offense? You have such a teensy imagination for such a strapping man!' Other actors in the class can make up dialogue at the drop of a hat. But me: I freeze. Each time she critiques me I get more uptight. 'The theater is not a place for acting!' šays Antoinette. 'No, no, no; it is a place for *re*acting! '" Bob's zesty French accent and fluttering hands were completely at odds with his mammoth scale.

Walter tried an experiment. "That's a great imitation! Let's hear more."

Bob cleared his throat and shifted on the couch. "Oui," he replied. "How iz zee Fresca, Wall-tar?" One wooden sentence was all it took to prove Bob's improvisational shortcomings beyond a doubt, and Walter, who smiled politely, was moved to resume the foot rub with deep, consoling strokes.

"See," sighed Bob. "Once I think I'm acting, I can't. It's like the centipede, or the caterpillar, or whatever it was that forgot how to walk."

"Centipede," said Walter.

"At this rate, I'll probably work at the Hammer for the rest of my life. The trouble is, bouncing's like ballet: I can't see myself doing it when I'm fifty."

"You call it 'bouncing'?" asked Walter.

"What else would I call it? 'Portal management'?"

"You're quick," said Walter.

"Right," said Bob. "Until I'm asked to improvise."

Walter pulled on Bob's toes, the cartilage cracking.

"What if I get called in for a cold reading? Or have to ad-lib during a play? You've got to admit this is one whopping problem. What can I do?"

Bob was right; as long as he couldn't trust his instincts, he'd be one among a throng of mediocre actors, replaceable as grains of rice. Walter knew the value of spontaneity; before he moved to Hollywood, he'd taken Noah Carmichael's controversial workshop, Elastic Theatrics. Noah thought it pointless to actually mount productions, since drama was a state of mind. Instead, he favored theater games, which often gravitated from his shabby storefront in the East Village and into the streets and subways and all-night coffee shops of Manhattan. Noah directed, or, as he preferred to put it, "urged possibilities," from the sidelines, his voice booming, his words still hot from the forge of inspiration. For two years, Walter never read, or acted in, a play. But he had stopped traffic on Eighteenth Street with a round of imaginary badminton, had grown hoarse vocalizing the sounds of his internal organs from the top of the Empire State Building, and had talked into a broken pay phone as if he were speaking to a dying wife.

As zealous as Walter had been about Carmichael's approach over, say, Uta Hagen's or Stanislavsky's, he'd begun to lose faith one night during an exercise at Grand Central Station. The actors had flung each other amid the commuters and they froze wherever they fell, waiting to be reanimated on a cue from Noah. Walter lay on the cold marble floor, watched men and women striding by, and while destinations blazed on a huge electric sign, he ached to feel himself buttoned in a suit, bound to a schedule, weighed down by a briefcase. *If I were one of these people,* he thought, *I'd step over myself and race for a train.*

Those times with Noah were far behind (when recalling what he'd done in public, Walter wished he'd learned to be more self-conscious instead of less) and he never would have guessed that he'd one day have reason to suggest a theatric, elastic or not. But Bob leaned over the edge of the couch, face plaintive, biceps swelling as he wrung his hands.

"I know an exercise you might try," said Walter. Noah had resorted to the Fall whenever the group's improvisations turned stale or premeditated; he considered it a desperate measure, a kind of artistic defibrillation. Noah swore the exercise prodded an actor to relinquish control, to give his body—which Noah called, somewhat salaciously, the exquisite instrument—over to chance.

"Show me," said Bob, rising to his feet. He tilted his head from side to side and limbered his shoulders with slow rotations, breathing from his diaphragm. Peering up from the floor, Walter watched Bob ready himself, willing to do whatever it took to better his craft. Regardless of Antoinette's admonitions and the dead-end job that paid for her classes, Bob still hoped to become an actor, the exemplary man whom life speaks through, like a clear sentence or a megaphone. Walter supposed that Bob hadn't yet racked up enough disappointments—futile auditions, countless call-backs, humiliating roles—to think himself either unlucky or deluded. Like numberless others, like Walter himself, Bob had come to Hollywood from a city now distant and unfamiliar, and he'd suffer his stubborn dedication until it had been thoroughly spent, or rewarded in such rare and paltry ways that, years from now, when change was too late, Bob would barely recall whom he'd hoped to become and why he'd decided to move here in the first place.

And so Walter stood. "Turn around," he said to Bob, "arms at your sides. Now shut your eyes and listen closely. You must trust your body to do what it wants, no matter how extreme. I'll be standing right behind you."

Silhouetted against the window, his back to Walter, Bob nodded and took a deep breath.

"Falling leaves," intoned Walter. "Falling water. Falling off the wagon. Falling for a joke." No one could rival Noah's hypnotic free associations, but Walter gave it all he had. "Falling from favor, from honor, from grace . . ."

Listening intently, Bob began to shift on his haunches, his body swaying back and forth. The length of him was suggestible, and also the breadth. "Pratfall. Nightfall. The fall of man . . ." The more Bob succumbed to gravity, the more dramatic Walter became.

Clouds drifted above the hillsides, bottom-heavy with pale light. Right about now, Paramount was beginning to stir. Henry, the guard, would check his clipboard in the same officious, distracted manner he had for years, waving cars and vans through the gate. Soon, slumped in her chair at the commissary, Janet would nervously stir her coffee, wondering where Walter was as she thumbed through yet another script, one of hundreds that came from the mailroom, from the desks of readers and secretaries, from the knapsacks of breathless messengers whose helmets bore decals of winged feet. This morning the stories would arrive as always, and no matter how fine or mundane or far-fetched, none would capture a dawn such as this or an act like the one Walter's longing had prompted.

He shucked off his jacket, tossed it aside; Bob was a lot of man to catch and Walter had to be unencumbered. Poised to lunge forward, he opened his arms. "Falling stars, prices, rocks . . ." Bob began to teeter steeply, his muscles and tendons surrendering, a fierce, inward grip letting go.

what to name the baby

1.

Laura steadied herself against the Winnebago's kitchenette and filled a glass from the tap. Eucalyptus trees flicked past the window, and in the yellowing pastures that lay behind them, horses grazed in the sun. She took a sip and touched her bulging stomach, hoping the metallic-tasting water wasn't bad for the baby. Just yesterday, she'd glimpsed her child in a sonogram, a gauzy, nameless girl curled into herself and floating on the video screen. *Little bean,* she'd thought, shivering as the technician drew the cold wand across her belly.

Her father turned from the passenger seat, a map of California spread on his lap. "Kit's a cute name," he shouted over the rumble of the motor.

"Kit's more of a boy's name," said Laura, lowering herself onto the banquette. Her knees were rubbery and unpredictable, gravity a nagging force she couldn't ignore. She hated the slippery vinyl seats and how she had to brace herself to keep from tipping over like a sack of cement whenever Booth steered the Winnebago through a sharp curve or came to a sudden stop. "I want her to have a name that's, like, totally female."

"Estrogenette?" Booth suggested. His eyes caught hers in the rearview mirror.

Laura knew he was joking, but it made her feel foolish. Unable to think of a comeback, she retaliated with the one thing that bothered Booth most: silence. Her father's lover was a poet. During the three years Booth and her dad had lived together, he'd tried to charm her with clever wordplay. For Laura, the only thing stranger than Booth's profession, if you could even call it that, was the fact that he made money at it. Money given by trusts and institutions with fancy, hyphenated names.

"When I was growing up," said her father, "there was a girl in my sixth-grade class whose last name was Force, and her parents, who were civil engineers, named her after the Erie Canal."

"Erie Force," said Booth. "That's spooky."

"I kind of like it," said Laura. Booth and her father looked at each other. "Maybe a kid with an unusual name grows up to be an unusual person." Once she said it, the theory sounded true. "I want my baby to have a unique destiny. If anybody can understand that," she persisted, "it should be you two."

"Frank, our bohemian credentials are being questioned." Booth reached out and squeezed her father's thigh.

Laura stiffened. She wondered if she would ever get used to the two of them holding hands during a movie, or bumping shoulders as they pushed a shopping cart, or hugging in the airport when Booth returned from an out-of-town reading. She'd visited them often since discovering she was pregnant (thanks to a home pregnancy test whose name, Clear Blue Easy, Booth had written in the notebook he always carried with him), and though she appreciated their willingness to cook Sunday dinners, contribute money to her obstetric bills, and drive her back to her apartment after dark, their kindness couldn't erase the discomfort she felt at the sight of two fifty-year-old men acting as infatuated as newlyweds. She'd long ago asked herself if she was jealous—after Ben walked out on her, all sorts of miserable, stingy emotions were possible—but she was genuinely happy that her father had found someone to love. Her wince was visceral and involuntary, as hard to stifle as a sneeze. The first time it happened, Frank had been clearing the dinner table when he bent to kiss the top of Booth's head, both of them turning in time to see Laura's eyes widen. It didn't help that, ever since then, Frank was as chaste as a choirboy in Laura's presence; Booth was the one who initiated a hug or a pat while Frank beamed with pleasure but kept his hands to himself. Instead of sparing Laura embarrassment, her father's restraint made her feel like a prude, the kind of coddled, stodgy girl she actively disliked.

"Hey," shouted Booth, pointing to a sun-bleached billboard. "Aerial Tramway. That would make a lovely name." Booth laughed at his own joke and rolled down the window, the breeze thrashing his silver hair. Every now and then he'd turn and contemplate her father. Laura had to admit that Booth was handsome, his green eyes lively, age spots mottling the backs of his hands like the markings of some exotic animal. Her disapproving silences and contrary remarks never seemed to faze Booth, and this, along with his imposing height, made him all the more stately and self-possessed. Still, she appreciated him as a woman would, and it was hard for her to imagine this same appreciation between two men, especially two older men, without there being something comical about it, like a movie she'd once seen in which the doddering granddads turned out to be fags, mooning over each other while the audience, including Laura, roared with laughter.

A sleepy, fertile odor rose from the fields and wafted through the window. Laura slipped off her sandals and lay back on the banquette. The extra-large T-shirt felt snug against her breasts, the elastic waistband of her stretch pants scoring a pink impression in her flesh. Propping her swollen ankles atop her duffel bag, Laura tried to imagine a world in which Booth and her father would be an ordinary couple: she pictured two men walking arm in arm toward a photogenic sunset; a ballroom in which dashing, tuxedoed financiers twirled and dipped one another on the dance floor; a couple of male retirees sitting on the same side of a booth at Denny's, ordering omelets from a single menu. Pretty weird stuff, she thought. Then again, it had been almost as weird to imagine sex between her mother and her father. In fact, when a playmate first broke the news about the mechanics involved in Laura's conception, she'd scoffed at her friend for believing something so silly and gross, and the little girl, suddenly doubtful, had begun to cry.

The baby shifted, and Laura blurted an oh of surprise. These days, the movements within her womb were blunt with elbows and knees, insistent taps for attention impossible to mistake for a cramping muscle or a hunger pang. It pleased her to think that, at any given moment, her cells were dividing, her blood and breath turning into nourishment. This internal work went on day and night, fueled more by her patience than her will. Even while riding in a Winnebago, idle and bloated and prone to daydreams, Laura could say that, physiologically speaking, she was a busy woman.

She closed her eyes, the bumps in the highway a blunted percussion. As she sank into a nap—the heavy, hormonal sleep that overwhelmed her several times a day—she listened to Booth make up strange names, a game in which her father had to guess the character's fates.

"Marble Obelisk," said Booth.

Frank folded the crackling map. "He's a Greek tycoon."

"Pearl Tapioca."

"The poor thing sells matchsticks."

"And wears a tattered shawl," Booth added.

Pearl, thought Laura, and the second before she lost herself to sleep, she saw an oyster yawning at the bottom of the sea.

Helium balloons had bobbed in the air above the RV dealership. Frank and Booth dashed across the asphalt and examined one boxy motor home after another. Booth paused repeatedly and jotted the names of the vehicles in his notebook. Laura had lagged behind, squinting against the sun, wondering how on earth Roust-About and Hi-Road and American Cruiser would figure in a poem. She was just beginning to show back then and had no trouble hoisting herself up the steps of a Winnebago, following Booth and her father. Despite curtains and throw pillows and woodlike laminates, the interior felt as echoey and impersonal as the inside of a tin can. Booth went directly to the driver's seat and tried the horn. "That's an awfully feeble toot," he said, "for so much metal." Intent on a well-equipped kitchen, her father twisted the timer on the microwave, peeked into the miniature refrigerator, and tested the latches on the cabinet doors. When her father and mother had been married, Frank performed the typical manly chores, like changing the Pontiac's oil and weatherproofing the deck. It amazed Laura to think that so many of his wishes—to cook the perfect bouillabaisse or pick out another man's ties—had lain dormant during her girlhood. In Booth's company, her father mugged, cracked jokes, and illustrated his stories with sweeping gestures, a more pliant and eccentric man than the dad she thought she knew.

A salesman knocked on the door of the Winnebago. Laura let him in, struck by his tangy aftershave and glossy black hair. "I see you've discovered our most popular model," he said, launching into a pitch about the power train, reinforced chassis, and catalytic converter. Frank and Booth went about their investigations, barely listening. The more their attention flagged, the more talkative the salseman became. "Young man," Booth finally interrupted, "Mr. Russo and I are looking, if I may be direct, for a love nest on wheels, and aesthetics mean much more to us than mechanical details, which we are merely pretending to comprehend. While we admire your knowledge and obvious enthusiasm, you would do well to let us cluck and fuss like the old hens we are determined to be." The salesman, as speechless as a valedictorian in a nightmare, turned to Laura. Booth had just received the Walbern-Holt Prize from the Western Academy of Poets, which carried with it a five-thousand-dollar honorarium, and Laura wished she could explain that Booth was riding high, more persnickety and forward than normal. She shrugged, and the salesman straightened his tie, winking at Laura before he left.

Laura cherished his momentary interest. Even passing flirtations helped her believe that Ben's leaving wasn't such a calamity, that she might someday have a future with another man. But no sooner had she bounced on the foldout bed than she remembered Ben's freckled shoulders, his narrow hips, and the urgent, boyish whimper that escaped him when he entered her. Boyishness was the trait that charmed and finally exasperated her. When he sang his folk songs, Ben's voice cracked with youthful indignation over America's chaos and hypocrisy, yet the entire time he lived in her apartment, he never bothered to hang up his clothes or take out the trash. Ben was probably sitting in some coffeehouse right now, plucking his guitar—it galled Laura to think of him singing a ballad about heartbreak—chestnut bangs hanging over his forehead while some gullible, pretty girl sipped a cappuccino and listened. Wrenching as they were, divorce or a spouse's death couldn't be any worse than waking up one morning to discover you've been abandoned. Ben didn't so much as leave a note. Nothing except for a few guitar picks scattered like arrowheads throughout her apartment. There she was with the rest of her life to wonder what went wrong. She told herself she was better off without him, but every time she looked in a mirror, she saw the woman he left behind instead of the girl she was before they met.

"It reeks of plastic in here," said Laura. She rose from the bed and opened a window. As far as motor homes were concerned, Laura thought people moved around too much as it was. Her childhood home in Hollywood had been sold long ago. Catherine, her mother, had moved to the Central Valley to live with her boyfriend, a husky surveyor with a dense black beard. Despite the fact that Dell did his best to be macho and argumentative, he reminded Laura of a circus bear, lumbering and tame, avid for snacks. Her mother, in fact, referred to Dell's hairy arms as his front legs. Laura was still getting used to the flirtatious, bantering tone of Catherine's new relationship. "It's a big plus that Dell couldn't possibly turn out to be gay," she recently told Laura. "The lughead lives to get a rise out of women. Namely me. You can't imagine how much we enjoy putting each other in our places; that way, we each have a place to be put into. By the way," she added, "tell your father that Dell thinks the Winnebago is a great idea. Of course, he'd probably think a covered wagon was even better." When Booth and her father had bought a house close to Laura, she'd thought of it as compensation for her mother's move. But now they were committing themselves to travel, and she worried that, after the baby was born, they might drive off to who knew where.

"Daddy," she said, "are you sure you want to wander around the country like a Gypsy?"

"We'll use the motor home for vacations, honey. Booth can bring along his notebook and write. The three, no, the four of us could go to Big Sur; we'll show the baby her very first redwood."

"It's vital to grasp one's place in nature," mused Booth, struggling to open the roof vent. "As long as you don't have to rough it."

Believe me, thought Laura, *I've grasped my place in nature.* She rose from the bed and undid the top button of her jeans; she'd grown too plump for them overnight. It was a solace and a terror, this prospect of being forever attached to a person who entered the world from inside you.

"If you'd asked me a couple of years ago," said her father, looking around, "I couldn't have imagined myself shopping for a motor home. The design goes against every principle I learned in architecture school."

"Think of it as the logical product of modernism," said Booth. "It's efficient, mass-produced, and adaptable. From the right perspective, Frank, a motor home is quite avant-garde. But without the pretense."

"Where does he come up with these things?" marveled Laura's father.

"I give up," said Laura. "Where?"

The Winnebago had stopped on the side of the road. Laura awoke slowly, the air around her warm and still. Pinned beneath the live weight of her stomach, she balked at the idea of sitting upright. The adage about eating for two applied to sleeping as well; these days sleep was fraught and exhausting, a horizontal marathon. As she heaved herself up, her lower back ached and tiny dots swarmed in the corners of her eyes.

Booth heard her stir and turned from the driver's seat. He'd been hunched over, writing, and he looked at her with foggy curiosity, a man straddling the world in his notebook and the world at hand. "We ran out of gas," he said, pushing his bifocals up the bridge of his nose. "Frank hitched a ride. There's a gas station in the next town. He should be back soon." Squeezing between the bucket seats, Booth went to the sink and poured Laura a glass of water. "Are you okay?" he asked, holding out the glass. Laura nodded, though she felt strangely constricted, as if she'd grown too big for her skin. She sipped the bitter water.

"You'd think I'd have read the owner's manual by now." Booth sat beside her, fanning himself with his notebook. "I thought the reserve tank would get us a hundred miles or so."

"What about the gas canisters in the back?"

"Those are for gas? I thought they were for lemonade."

It took Laura a moment to realize he was joking. "Where are we?" she asked.

Booth opened his notebook and read, "'We found ourselves between Aurora and Newton.'"

"You wrote that in your notebook?"

"I . . . it seemed to mean something."

"Like?"

"I'd have to keep writing to find out."

"Read me something else."

He thumbed through the pages. "'Possible Dust Clouds.' That was a sign I saw when your father and I drove to the Mojave Desert. It would make a fantastic title for something, don't you think?"

Laura blinked, studying Booth. How could her mother and father have ended up with such different men? Did love have some logic she was just too blind or unlucky to grasp?

The two of them sat side by side in silence. Laura couldn't recall spending time alone with Booth during any of her visits to their house; faithful to the page, he often excused himself to read or write, leaving Laura and her dad to wash the dishes or take an after-dinner walk. She folded her hands in her lap, pressed her thighs together in order to ease her aching back. If there was one thing Laura hated, it was searching for something to say, the way your brain became a big echoing vault, your entire life too humdrum to mention. A poet, she believed, wouldn't have that problem. But Booth appeared awkward, too; he clutched his notebook and cleared his throat, at a rare loss for words.

Laura shifted her weight, trying to find a comfortable position, but pain pooled through her in nauseating waves. She struggled to her feet when sitting became unbearable, using Booth's shoulder for support. Booth stood, too. He seemed to read her face rather than look at it, and he took her by both hands. For one woozy second, she thought they were about to dance. "Laura?" he asked. Just as she began to buckle, Booth grabbed her by the waist and draped her arm around his neck. She wouldn't have been able to remain standing without him; she was afraid he might let go, afraid that if the pain continued she'd lose control of her bladder or bowels. She rested her head against his chest.

The pain subsided long enough for Laura to mumble instructions. She wasn't sure the words made sense. Booth sat her down on the banquette, ransacking her duffel bag until he found the dog-eared book. "It's my lower back," she said; if she'd had breath to spare, she might have laughed at the sheer futility of expecting Booth to make a diagnosis based on four words. He adjusted his glasses, squinting at the index. To Laura's surprise, Booth yelped "Backache!" and quickly turned to the right page. The illustration on the cover—a pink fetus nestled in the cross section of a womb—trembled in his hands.

How could this happen now, on the way to her mother's? Laura had planned to spend the last weeks of her pregnancy sprawled in a BarcaLounger, fussed over by her mom, watching TV and reading the magazines Dell would bring home for her, the birth overseen by a doctor who, according to Catherine, was the best ob-gyn in the Central Valley. Laura had forwarded her medical records, sublet her apartment in L.A. This period of leisure was supposed to end in a haze of anesthetic ("Get an epidural," her mother urged her. "Natural childbirth is for wildlife"), the baby's arrival a painless labor. Now she might have to squat and curse and give birth the hard way, her father's lover the midwife.

"Get down on all fours!" shouted Booth, persuasive by way of his growing panic. With his help, she settled herself onto the floor. "Rock back and forth. Don't arch your back."

Laura did as she was told, head hanging down. "Better," she whimpered. "Should I time my contractions? I'm not sure they're contractions."

She heard Booth frantically thumb through the index. "What am I looking for?"

A cramp suddenly wrung her like a rag. "'Guts on Fire' for Christ's sake!" She clenched her teeth, rocking and grunting. "I'm sorry," she said, unable to turn her head far enough to see if he was still standing beside her. Sweat prickled the surface of her skin. She tried not to cry. "Booth?"

"If it gets any worse, lower your head and keep your . . . posterior in the air. I'm going to flag down some help. I'll be right outside, Laura. Shout if you need me."

After the metal door clanked shut, Booth's absence hovered above her, as cold and remote as a star. She wanted her father. Her mother. Someone. *Once the baby comes,* thought Laura, *I won't be alone.* She reached between her legs, dreading the slickness of blood or the shock of water, but her fingers were dry when she drew back her hand. Laura told herself that she and the baby would both be safe. As frightened as she was, the voice in her head was tempered and maternal. *Someday,* she thought, rocking back and forth, *Pearl will listen to this story and laugh.*

2.

Booth flailed his arms at an approaching car and lunged into the middle of the road. He didn't realize he was waving *The Birth Book* in one hand until the driver, a stout woman in a floral dress, squinted at the pink fetus before speeding off. Her Cadillac spewed a cloud of exhaust. "If you can read this," said her bumper sticker, "you're too damn close." He visored his eyes with the book, checked the highway in both directions, and willed another car to come along. Mirages of water shivered on the highway, and a stable hugged the far horizon. *The breadth of the empty sky oppressed him.* This was one of the more evocative phrases he'd thought of all day, and he felt both guilty and exhilarated to think that he could mine words from such dire circumstances.

Booth ran to the Winnebago and peered through a window to check on Laura, still rocking on her hands and knees. The T-shirt had ridden up her back, exposing the globe of her stomach, the curve of a pale breast. He backed away, returned to the road. As a teenager, Booth had heard that homosexuals hated women; but even back then, he suspected that how he felt about women had nothing whatever to do with hate. Or fear. Or indifference. Not until decades later, while composing a poem, had he found the right words: "Whose soft appeal / Releases me from longing."

A pickup truck appeared in the distance. Booth held the book at his side and waved in steady, emphatic strokes. The driver, a young woman wearing a pair of faded overalls and a tie-dyed T-shirt, slowed to a stop. Her short hair, which looked as though it had been cut by a blindfolded barber, was the color of grape soda. Hoops, chains, and cheap trinkets dangled from the piercings along the rim of her ear. She rolled down the passenger window. "What's the trouble?"

"My daughter," Booth began. "Daughter" was the first word that came to mind; once he'd said it, paternal sentiment flooded his chest, then an even greater desperation. "We need your help," he told the girl, gripping the door as if to prevent her from driving away. He had to shout over the rumble of the idling engine and the yips of a black Labrador who scrabbled in the truck bed.

Laura let loose a held breath when the two of them entered the Winnebago. She struggled to sit upright, damp hair clinging to her face.

Rachel McMullen bent down toward Laura and introduced herself. "Looks like your timing's a little off."

"I'll say," said Laura. Her rescuer was young and female; Laura required no other credentials. Limp and compliant, she let the two of them hoist her up and guide her outside.

"Don't expect an easy ride in this old heap," said Rachel, helping Booth lay Laura on the truck bed. "The Valley Clinic is across the road from my kennel in Newton. Dan, who's on duty during the week, is mostly an ophthalmologist. But he's brought people back from heart attacks and mended plenty of broken bones."

Booth dashed back to the Winnebago, scrawled in his notebook, "Gone to Valley Clinic, Newton," and left it open on the driver's seat. He signed it with a "B," like the notes he left for Frank around the house, domesticity's updates and endearments. When he returned to the truck, Rachel was scratching the dog's chest, telling Laura how Smudge's mother, a haughty purebred, ate the litter's afterbirth. "Afterbirth is rich in nutrients and gives the bitch a big dose of protein." Laura nodded vaguely, clinging to any distraction.

The truck creaked on its springs as Booth settled himself beside Laura. He'd brought along the duffel bag and helped her rest her head atop it. She closed her eyes against the sun. "We're ready," he said, bracing his back against the cab.

Rachel ground the gears and stepped on the gas. The truck lurched into motion, spewing gravel from its rear tires. Smudge's legs splayed out from under him. After clattering to his feet, he trotted toward Laura and sniffed her crotch, transfixed by the scents of impending labor. Laura seemed too tired to mind. Booth held *The Birth Book* above her face; it made a jittery patch of shade. "My awning," said Laura. The odd phrase, Booth believed, was meant to please him. With her forehead tensed, she looked like Frank when he scrutinized a blueprint. Booth stroked her shoulder. Smudge sat beside her and, ears flapping back, long pink tongue lolling from his muzzle, squinted into the wind.

Sky and farmland streaked by on either side of the highway. Booth hoped he hadn't made a mistake by putting Laura's fate in a stranger's hands. He craned around, peering into the cab. A chewed-up tennis ball rolled back and forth across the dashboard. From the rearview mirror there dangled a plastic Statue of Liberty that had been zipped into a doll's sequined cocktail dress. And in front of him, through the tinted glass, rose the back of their rescuer's purple head.

At first Booth dismissed the sight as some kind of hallucination, a trick played by wishfulness or overworked nerves. Rachel's truck passed half a prefabricated house being towed in the opposite direction, its interior visible for an instant behind huge, transparent sheets of plastic. Wandering among its empty rooms was a man who looked uncannily like Frank, holding a bright red gas can in his hand. By the time Booth realized he'd spotted his lover, it was too late to call out, to tell Frank to turn around, to let him know where his daughter was headed. In a flash the house had sailed past them, its bold sign, "Wide Load," shrinking fast. The house seemed to hover above the road, as if skimming the earth to find its foundation.

Booth was still looking down the highway, dumbstruck, when Laura rolled onto her back and hissed through clenched teeth. Water seeped from between her legs and advanced like a shadow. Her pant legs darkened, the quilt soaking through. Booth banged his fist against the rear window, and the startled dog slouched as Rachel sped up. "Hold on," he told Laura. They clung to each other, lush fields giving way to one-story houses, modest shops, a row of brick municipal buildings.

By the time they barreled into the clinic's parking lot, Laura was writhing in Booth's lap, clutching her stomach, testing the strength of her vocal cords. "Where's Ben?" she yelled, shuddering with laughter. "I'll give that fucker something to sing about." She seemed to thrive on the power of delirium, as if it were the last, brash resource of her exhausted body. Booth tried to remain sensible, but he found himself hiccupping with airless giggles when Laura looked up and, in what he feared was absolute earnestness, promised him the pick of the litter.

Dr. Dan met them in the waiting room, alerted to their arrival by the receptionist, a small watchful woman who held open the door. Dan seemed unperturbed by Laura's state, and by Booth's as well; both of them wore the same pained grin, as if they'd been rushed to the clinic for the antidote to a private joke. For Laura's sake, Booth wanted to see stethoscopes, squirting hypodermics, all the shiny, sterilized tools of medical aid and expertise. But there was only Dan's white lab coat to put him at ease. While Dan settled Laura into a wheelchair and checked her pulse, Rachel told him how, while searching for strays, she'd spotted their motor home on the highway.

"Dan," bellowed Laura, gripping his wrist, "can you get this baby out of me right away?"

"Only with your help," he said, releasing the foot brake and wheeling Laura down the pale green hallway. Rachel and Booth raced after them. "I don't think we're looking at Braxton Hicks," Dan shouted over his shoulder. "It's not uncommon for back labors to come on with a wallop." Despite his sober, knowing voice, the doctor was young and padded with baby fat, his eyes an almost frivolous blue. Booth wanted to shout, "Show me your diplomas!" "It would be best if you two made yourselves comfortable in the waiting room. I'll do everything I can to expedite the delivery, but this may take a while." He backed the wheelchair through a door marked "Medical Staff Only." Laura clutched her stomach and grimaced.

Booth stood there as the door clicked shut. Since he wasn't related to Laura, not in the usual sense at least, he had no legal claim to her supervision; father-in-law, uncle—his connection had no name. Laura's visits to the house made Frank happy, and ever since they'd lived together, Booth's happiness had hinged on his lover's. Late at night, after they'd driven Laura home, he and Frank would spoon-breathe in bed, a seam of heat between their naked bodies, while Frank recounted one of Laura's clever or funny or troubling remarks. Booth had long understood that he could listen with magnanimity and offer wise advice precisely because Laura wasn't his daughter. He could drift into an easy sleep while Frank churned beneath the blankets, mulling over the mystery, the lifelong burden of his only child.

Booth paced around the waiting room. Rachel fidgeted in a vinyl chair. Every now and then the receptionist would stop reading, reach into her seemingly bottomless purse, and offer them a jawbreaker, aspirin, or—somewhat ominously, Booth thought—a Kleenex. "This room is getting awfully small," said Rachel, leaping to her feet. "Why don't we go across the street. There's a coffeemaker at the kennel. They can call us the second there's news."

"Go ahead," said Booth. "You've done more than enough for us already. Besides, I'm waiting for someone."

"You mean, the baby?"

"No. Laura's father."

Rachel pointed. "You're Laura's father."

"Not quite."

"You're—what?—her stepfather?"

"I live with her father. Laura doesn't have a husband."

The receptionist peered at them over her paperback book.

Rachel made silent calculations, then snapped her fingers, a pop of comprehension. "You and Laura's father are lovers! That's fantastic."

"As in, 'unbelievable'?"

"No, as in, 'That's really great.'"

"How do you know?" asked Booth. "Maybe we're one of those bickering old couples who make each other miserable."

The receptionist dispensed with the pretense of reading. She propped her chin on her palm and listened, a jawbreaker tucked in her bulging cheek.

"You're in love," said Rachel. "I can see it in your face. You can afford to be sarcastic because you're actually happy."

But as he and Rachel left the clinic—she'd talked him into coffee and insisted they call the highway patrol—Booth was anything but happy. Being in love, in fact, seemed incompatible with happiness, since love carried with it the constant threat of separation. Shouldn't Frank have filled the tank and found the town by now?

Smudge sat at attention in the truck bed. When Rachel whistled, he hurtled over the tailgate and bounded to her side. The three of them crossed Newton's main street, a picture postcard of quaint architecture, sparse traffic, and wide blue sky. Booth thought, *nostalgia's last outpost*, and reflexively patted his pocket for a pen.

As Rachel unlocked the door, whimpers, howls, and barks detonated inside the kennel. Booth felt his body clench against the noise, a unanimous urgency without words. They had to walk through the echoing gauntlet of dogs in order to get to Rachel's office. Booth followed behind with Smudge, watching as Rachel reached between the bars to stroke a sickly shepherd mix, or to scratch the belly of a stubby mutt who greeted her by leaping onto its hind legs. Rachel cooed and whispered to one white mop of a lapdog, but she couldn't coax it any closer; its wariness suggested to Booth a life of plumped pillows and gourmet food, followed by a fall from grace—skulking through alleys, scrounging in the trash, napping with one eye open.

Booth squinted at the index cards taped to the cages. They listed the age, sex, and breed of each dog. The spaces where their names should have been struck Booth as gaping voids, sad blanks. While continuing down the corridor, he christened each animal under his breath: Carlotta, Tidbit, Slurp, St. Mange.

Thanks to Rachel's ministrations, a lull soon fell over the kennel. Dogs lapped at bowls of water or poked their leathery noses between bars. She led Booth into a small cinder-block office, switched on the light, and dialed the highway patrol. Rachel explained that she ran the kennel and asked the dispatcher to put out a call about the Winnebago. Booth took the receiver and gave the dispatcher his license plate number, repeating it twice and making her promise that, when the motor home was found, an officer would escort the driver to Newton. "His name is Frank Russo, and his daughter is giving birth at the Valley Clinic as we speak. Please hurry before it gets dark. The poor dear has a pitiful sense of direction." Moved by a pang of guilt, Booth added, "Although spacially speaking, he's really quite sophisticated."

Once he hung up, he sank into a chair matted with dog hair. Smudge planted himself beside Booth, as if to offer a sedative of warm fur and steady breath. He stroked the dome of Smudge's head, both their faces inclined toward Rachel. She poured the coffee, her prodigious earrings catching the light. "Do you and Frank have pets?" she asked, handing him a Dalmatian-spotted mug.

3.

In his life as an architect, Frank Russo had walked through countless houses under construction, but never one that was moving, uprooted. Doors and kitchen cupboards were taped shut to keep them from swinging. Jarred by bumps in the road, gypsum wallboard sloughed off a fine dust. Frank paused in the living room and saw, through rustling sheets of plastic, miles of landscape slipping past.

Only moments ago, gas can in hand, he'd been trying without success to thumb a ride in front of the Shell station in Aurora. All the while the owner, who couldn't leave the station unattended, leaned against a pump and shouted "So much for that one" every time a car barreled by. Both he and Frank were startled when a huge truck, prefabricated house in tow, came to a halt by the side of the road, air brakes exhaling. A father, mother, and four children leaped from the cab, shaking cramps from their hands and feet. The kids ran to buy soft drinks while the father, fanning his face with a baseball cap, explained to Frank that he was moving his family to Anaheim, where the other half of their house was waiting. The mother, dressed in a pink sweat suit, said she felt sorry for Frank and insisted they stop to give him a ride. In a quaint improvisation of hospitality, she lifted a flap of plastic, urged him to make himself at home, then herded her family back into the cab. He almost toppled over when the house took off.

Frank explored the jostling rooms. As a boy, he'd loved visiting model homes in the Hollywood Hills, comforted by certain touches—school pennants, a table set for dinner, fanned magazines—that gave the illusion a family lived there. His, he'd pretend. Standing inside those tableaux of home made him feel like a husband and father, like the man he feared he might never become.

Now he'd been divorced for five years, a new life starting to form around him like a floor plan embracing empty space. He was proud that he and Catherine could be civil with each other, glad she'd found a suitable match in burly, cantankerous Dell.

As for Laura, her adult life had been compounded by one abandonment after another, and she wore her disappointment like a badge. Frank was determined to compensate his daughter for her losses, to prove his allegiance however he could. Laura might never feel completely at ease when he and Booth touched, but he hoped she might return his allegiance despite her discomfort. That, he thought, would be enough.

Frank didn't mind having to limit physical contact with Booth when Laura was around; he preferred clandestine touches in public. Sometimes he saw boys strolling arm in arm down Santa Monica Boulevard, or straining above a café table to meet in a brief, conspicuous kiss. As much as he envied their ease, such displays would have required of him a self-consciousness and courage that defeated the very purpose of touching, distracting him from the warmth of his lover's hands and lips. His desire for men had been tamped down for so long, and with such skill, that he'd turned "accidental" grazes and the sensual pressure of elbows and knees into a subtle, satisfying art. Booth was much braver about these things, likely to lean over and bite Frank's ear or massage his neck at a stoplight—attentions that felt too good to discourage, even if they made Frank nervous. Between the two of them, he figured, they did plenty of touching, obvious or not.

The family dropped him off at the stranded Winnebago and, after a couple of parting honks, they lurched away, the engine protesting its heavy load. He dashed across the desolate highway, gas can sloshing.

Stepping inside the Winnebago, Frank thought Booth and Laura might be hiding, planning to surprise him, though he couldn't imagine why. When he saw that Laura's duffel bag was gone, emptiness struck like a blow. He ran outside, called their names into quiet fields. His voice startled birds from the underbrush.

Frank finally found the message in Booth's notebook and filled the tank as fast as he could. He was breathing hard as he set off toward Newton, or where he imagined Newton to be. Relying on forward momentum was one thing, but if he overshot a single turn, he'd be forced to back this monster up and turn it around. Usually, the task of driving the Winnebago had fallen to Booth, while Frank became what Booth liked to call a decorative crew member. And now, the dashboard's unfamiliar buttons and sluggish brakes added to Frank's sense that he'd been sabotaged by circumstance. Wherever he looked, afternoon dimmed into evening, not a service station or person in sight. He told himself to stay calm—he'd been in charge before, had headed a household, was capable of finding a nearby town. But soon he was lost, blaming his lousy sense of direction, cursing the falling dominoes of longing that had brought him to the middle of nowhere, an aging homosexual alone in a motor home.

Since there wasn't any traffic to obstruct, Frank simply stopped the Winnebago in the middle of the road and unfolded a map. Busy squinting at minuscule names, he jumped when a highway patrolman, who appeared out of nowhere, rapped on the window and asked to see his driver's license. Frank handed it over. The cop scrutinized Frank's face as if he suspected that it, not the photograph, had been forged. "You're him, all right," the cop concluded.

*   *   *

Hands clamped on the steering wheel, Frank followed the speeding CHP officer over the crest of a hill. The patrol car's high beams tunneled into darkness. Scattered lights on the valley floor shimmered in waves of rising heat. A quick but steep descent toward Newton, where Frank was escorted down the town's main street. At the Valley Clinic, the patrol-man handed him over to Dan, who rushed him to a room where Laura lay propped up on a hospital bed, a baby in her pale arms. Frank kissed Laura's forehead, still damp from la-bor. He smelled the milky contentment in her skin, along with sour traces of strain. Instead of feeling that he'd finally found her, Frank felt as if it were he who'd been found—by Laura, her child, the luminous room. "Daddy," she said, fix-ing her exhausted eyes on the infant. Frank peered into the baby's face. Wrenched into a separate body, Pearl grimaced at the rude light, the endless air, her tiny, restless mouth tensed around a cry.

Daylight sifted through the canopy of branches. On either side of the winding road, the distance was almost opaque with red-woods. Frank steered the Winnebago through sharp turns with a caution and lassitude he thought of as sightseeing. Now and then he reached out the window and signaled an impatient driver to pass. Laura sat beside him and bounced the gurgling Pearl on her lap. Pearl took a swat at Laura's nose. "Bonk," said Laura. A grin wavered on the baby's face, her head unsteady on the stem of her neck.

Today was Pearl's first birthday, and Laura, in what Frank considered a feat of structural engineering, had packed her duf-fel bag with the baby's clothes, ointments, and toys, and stocked the small refrigerator with vanilla ice cream, a carrot cake Frank baked from scratch, and little jars of Pearl's favorite food, a pea-green pap with particles of ham.

"Don't you wish they made these for grown-ups?" Laura asked her father, patting the baby's flannel sleeper. She was amazed these days by all that filled the life of her child: the car seat with a built-in abacus, the adhesive tabs on Pampers. If Laura was unfocused before the baby's birth, the world now existed for one of two reasons, Pearl's delight or irritation; Laura's thoughts and actions all followed from there. As he watched his daughter bouncing Pearl, Frank was reminded that parents aren't much different from their infants—just as needy, as subject to hunger, as intent on the loved and hovering face.

He checked the rearview mirror and, seeing Booth fast asleep on the banquette, wondered whether it would be worth waking him for the scenery. "Overgrown," "green"—his own words wouldn't do; Frank wanted to hear what Booth would say, his unexpected turns of phrase changing the way Frank saw the forest. But Booth needed his rest. His mouth hung open, his expression nearly symmetrical, like the man Frank knew before the stroke.

Carlotta curled atop Booth's chest, rising and falling with his every breath. The dog's loyalty had been particularly keen during these months of rehabilitation; she constantly watched him, basked in his shadow, gingerly sniffed his fingers and shoes. She sulked whenever the two of them left the apartment for Booth's sessions with the speech therapist, then quivered and whimpered the second they returned, a furry nerve set off by his presence. When it came to "Daddy Frank," however, their foundling growled and shrank from his touch. That Carlotta was a fussy white lapdog hadn't helped endear her to

Frank, though this was exactly why Booth chose her. "Who else in a town as rustic as Newton is going to claim this little powder puff?" he'd asked Frank, a forlorn chorus barking in the background.

"He's got a point," Rachel had added. "Border collies and retrievers are the popular breeds around these parts."

"Most people would be too embarrassed to adopt her. Men especially. Her care requires the courage of a queen." Booth held the squirming dog against his chest. "There's no way to pass with a cockapoo."

From the moment they brought her home, Booth cultivated her girlish grooming. He tied a lavender bow on her topknot and bought her a gaudy rhinestone collar. "I'm restoring her to her former glory," he told Frank. Only after Booth fell ill was Frank impressed by the dog's devotion, fierce for a creature so pampered and small.

Carlotta leaped from Booth's chest as they pulled into the the Big Sur Picnic Grounds. She trotted toward the door and stood at attention, senses alert for whatever came next. Her movement roused Booth, whose face grew wakeful, one side sagging. He worked himself upright, touching his cheek to test it for sensation. Pearl heard him stirring and peekabooed over her mother's shoulder, several plump fingers bunched in her mouth. "I see a baby," said Booth. "Hello, baby." His words were halting, heavy with effort, but fond enough to make Pearl laugh and huff a saliva bubble.

The speech therapist had suggested that Booth speak one word at a time, in short declarative sentences rather than long ambitious ones that tended to fray or trail off. Aphasia had at first affected his comprehension as well as his speech, so this rule applied to Frank as well. "Until your friend recovers some

basic language skills," she advised him, "you might find it use-
ful to speak very slowly."

Booth said, "Like Dick and . . ."

Frank waited. "Jane," he said.

Hardest for Frank to accept had been those moments when
Booth struggled to find the right word. Blanks happened without warning, no matter how deliberately he formed a thought,
closing his eyes in concentration, stringing together beads of
meaning. When he failed to retrieve the word he needed, his
body stiffened, everything in him pitted against forgetfulness,
a lapse he would not allow. Only in the past month had there
occurred an improvement in Booth's powers of recall; he'd
suddenly pluck a word from silence, as surprised as if he'd
pulled a rabbit from a top hat. "My mind has gaps," he explained to Frank, "but my mouth wants to move."

Hefting Pearl in her arms, Laura stood in the parking lot,
gazing into the woods. Frank positioned himself outside the
Winnebago and helped Booth to the ground, supporting his
arm and back so that what might strike the casual onlooker as
the mere physics of assistance was in fact a set of messages
telegraphed by touch. They'd recently resumed having sex after months of doctor-ordered abstinence, every exertion straining the pulses within Booth's neck and wrists and groin, the
outposts of his pounding heart. Sometimes this reminder of
mortality made them tender, even timid. At other times they
made love with a death-defying abandon, then fell away from
each other's bodies, as satisfied as they were alive.

Still shy, especially in broad day, about the involuntary
downturn of his mouth and the crimson tissue beneath one
eye, Booth batted Frank away with his notebook. These days,
Booth opened it less often, but he carried it everywhere, just in

case. Shortly after Pearl was born, Booth had finished *Possible Dust Clouds;* Frank helped him edit the galleys, impressed by Booth's exactitude, his rigor with every syllable and image. Each page was a portal to his lover's inner life, a place inviting and forever separate.

Frank led his family on a walk into the woods. It only took a couple of steps before the conifers engulfed them, shade prevailing over everything in sight. Beneath their feet lay a moist, spongy carpet of mulch. Frank turned to check on Booth, whose expression was half inhabited by awe. Laura had slowed her pace to walk beside him. He gripped her elbow, relying on her balance to steady his. Frank took note of their proximity, their synchronized stride, but resisted appreciating it for fear that the act of observation might spoil a sight so rare. He continued to navigate the maze of vegetation—slender alders, velvety ferns. Carlotta rustled through the underbrush, then sprinted ahead of the straggling pack, stopping to yap as if at the audacity of such tall trees.

Soon they came to a halt, looking about, huddled in the midst of a green indifference. The dog raised her muzzle and sniffed the air. Recalling a long-ago promise, Frank took the baby from Laura's arms, and held her high above his head. "Redwoods," he said. But Pearl began to buck and fret. She couldn't take her big myopic eyes off the people gathered beneath her. No matter how much the three of them cajoled and burbled and pointed upward, the baby refused to lift her head, to turn away from human sound.

X

The DJ is sampling new cuts by Migraine and Rank Amateur when Nelson comes on to the drug. Every time a disc is dragged backward, the lyrics blur into a sweet, prolonged screech that's not much different from when they're sung forward. His eardrums have stopped hurting and the bass throbbing from overhead speakers, so amplified it's fuzzy, pelts the dance floor like a blizzard of lint. He can tell he's tweaked because he's staring at his feet. When he looks up, he can't find the shirtless boy he'd been dancing with, but he keeps the beat, keeps moving because it's too hard not to; he belongs to all and none of them at once, this mass agitation, this churning pack. He wants to take a running jump and slide across the humid room on the bare, glistening backs of his companions. Nelson lifts his T-shirt over his head and thinks that, once uncovered, his torso is going to light up the club, but by the time he wrenches his head from the neckhole, the idea is old. No sooner is he stripped to the waist than a kiss lands on the nape of his neck. Nelson turns to face a stranger. Very cute. Damp blades of hair fall across his forehead. Mouth framed in an oval goatee. Judging from the movement of his lips—words are buried miles below the music—the guy shouts "Pardon me" or "Party boy." Nelson doesn't hear or care. Next thing he knows is the thrilling, insolent plunge of a tongue, bitter from cigarettes.

By now, Nelson's neural transmitters are bathed in several days' worth of serotonin. The million synapses lacing his brain fire off pleasant messages. What he experiences is identical to the chemical composition of love, which occurs naturally given the right sensory triggers. The desire he's dreaded most of his life floods his bloodstream, animates his hands.

The last time an impulse to reach out and kiss a man struck him with such force, Nelson was ten, sitting on the rim of his parents' pool, dangling his legs in the deep end. All around him, concrete burned like clay from a kiln. The cool promise of water drew his older sister, Alma, and her husband-to-be from inside the house. Though Alma wore a bikini whose color their mother called shocking pink, it was Tiko's silky boxing trunks—prettier than anything he thought a man was supposed to wear—that Nelson found shocking. Alma and Tiko braved the hot pavement and took a running dive into the pool, but Tiko's body seemed to freeze, suspended in midair. Nelson stopped breathing: beautiful, the sunstruck muscles. Then water swallowed the soles of Tiko's feet, waves breaking the sunlight to bits.

Nelson watched as Tiko and his sister hugged at the bottom of the pool. Alma's long hair fanned out like seaweed, drifting on invisible currents. *Don't they need to breathe?* he wondered.

They might stay under and never come up. And just when he felt
a surge of worry, they shot to the surface and gulped for air,
treading water face to face, still drowning somehow, and
happy about it. Water slapped against Nelson's calves. He
found himself wishing that he was his sister.

"Pea," said Alma—that was what his family called him, because he was the youngest of six—"maybe you could get Tiko
some iced tea. There's a pitcher in the fridge." She nudged
Tiko's shoulder, tattooed with a dot the size of a dime, solid
blue. He paddled in place and looked at Nelson. "Buddy," he
said, in a voice that always got what it asked for, "I'm dry as
dust." As if in contradiction, droplets slid down his temples
and wet hair clung to his head. Nelson knew this was just an
excuse to get rid of him for a couple of minutes—what could
they do in a couple of minutes?—but now his future had this
in it: Tiko reaching up from the pool, half-naked and taking a
glass from his hand.

Nelson sighed and trudged toward the house, pretending
Alma's request was a burden. He made sure to push open the
screen door with a theatrical exasperation they would notice
from the pool, if they even bothered to look, and just as the
door sprang shut behind him, he heard a yelp that made him
wince. He spun around and saw Tiko standing on the other
side of the screen, clutching his face with massive hands. All
Nelson could think was that Tiko had followed him into the
house to use the bathroom or get a towel, and the screen door
must have slammed on his nose. He stifled a laugh at the in-
jury, crazy like in a cartoon. Tiko liked to brag that his nose had
been broken several times, so maybe once more would be doing him a favor. Then Tiko's fingers fell away and Nelson saw
the missing teeth.

"Ay, coño!" Tiko groaned. He barreled into the house and fell into a nearby chair, dazed as if in the corner of a ring. Nelson's mother would be mad that Tiko's wet trunks had soaked the upholstery, and this final flourish of trouble made Nelson want to cry. He would have, too, if Tiko hadn't opened his hand to reveal three teeth. They glowed like square, unearthly pearls. Nelson glanced back and forth from palm to mouth, frightened by the gaping spaces—all his fault. He had never felt sorrier for anything in his life. *Poor mouth,* thought Nelson. He remembered how his mother used to kiss his bruises when he took a tumble, drinking his hurt, making it hers. With this in mind—to make it better, to take it away—he reached toward Tiko and kissed him on the lips.

The blow seemed to come out of nowhere. Tiko's fist only grazed Nelson's cheek, but the impact was enough to knock him to the floor, where he trembled like water. Alma stood at the screen door, her face blazing with rage. At Tiko, Nelson thought at first. "You little idiot!" Alma bellowed. "It was a joke! They're Tiko's false teeth. He lost them in a fight." Framed in the doorway, stiff with disgust, she appeared older and more remote than the sister Nelson thought he knew, as though she'd left home long ago; it was hard to remember that they lived together and shared the same parents. He noticed the dot tattooed on Alma's shoulder (no matter where she and Tiko were, they connected at these indelible points), and the sight of it struck him like another punch.

Tiko brusquely nudged the missing teeth back into his mouth. Without so much as glancing at the boy—he would never look at Nelson the same way again—he followed Alma into the kitchen, where ice cubes chimed like faraway bells.

Nelson touched his aching jaw, moved it a little to see if it worked. Before he knew it (his head barely had time to clear), Tiko and his sister were married, living in another part of L.A. He suspected his kiss had driven them away, and so he believed, for years and years, that he deserved exactly what he got.

Tonight though, the music disproves it. Dancing beneath the speakers is like being shaken by a great voice. Even if he can't understand what it's saying, the volume is a kind of conviction, and the lyrics seem to come from inside his chest. It feels so good to grind his jaw, to feel the sleek enamel of his teeth. Tiko's blow couldn't be further from his thoughts. He dances the dance of pleasure and forgetting. He moves in sync with hundreds of others who will spend the night—deafening, endless—buzzed on drugs. When Nelson is high, he finds it easy to probe a stranger's mouth, and to feel his wanting boomerang back. He thinks of everything "X" can stand for: "X"'s in the eyes of men knocked senseless, kisses strung at the end of a letter. "X" is for the unknown man in his arms. Nelson and his partner embrace, in love for as long and bright as lightning before they drift toward someone else.

bit-o-honey

All day, while Ross's customers made small talk, snippets of hair raining down around them, he couldn't stop thinking about his father. Even that evening as he swept the floor, turned the sign in the window to "Closed", and bundled up the barber drapes he took home to wash, Ross kept coming back to his dad.

He'd meant to drive straight home after work, but the car made a sharp, last-minute turn and wound through narrow foothill roads. Tonight was Halloween, and a fittingly eerie sliver of moon had risen over Hollywood. Ross turned up Ridgecrest Avenue, a street where the houses stood far from the curb and walkways led to large front doors. Amber porch lights glowed through the trees. Pumpkins leered from front steps. Children who'd waited impatiently all day were spilling onto the sidewalks in costume, clutching paper bags at their sides and scavenging for candy.

Ross parked his car in front of Mrs. Hartounian's; she was his old next-door neighbor. He considered getting out and walking past his father's house; maybe he'd discover some clue to what had happened between them—a silhouette in a window, a stranger's car parked in the driveway, some sign of illness or dereliction. But he hated to think that his father might see him alone in the dark, a son who had nothing better to do than lurk in the street like a spy.

In the past year, Ross had called and hung up on his father at least a dozen times. Despite how childish he considered the act, the need to phone his father was as urgent as hunger, and when it struck, his body obeyed. As soon as he heard the familiar voice, Ross would cover the mouthpiece with his hand to mask the sound of his quickening breath. The silence that followed was a contest of wills. "Whoever this is," Mr. Gold finally blurted, "you better stop pestering me!" Ross would wince, depress the lever, and listen to the hum of the dial tone.

Occasionally, he'd reach the answering machine. "Hello. This is the telephone machine. I am not at home at this present time." He was saddened by his father's halting voice. More and more isolated since his retirement from the insurance firm, Mr. Gold had lost contact with other agents from the office, and had few friends as far as Ross knew. Still, the message's jolly, incongruous coda—"Have a nice day!"—filled Ross with fury. How dare he wish happiness to any stranger who happened to call, when he wouldn't even speak to his only son.

A boy and girl dressed in the pantaloons and eye patches of marauding pirates walked up the flagstone path to his old house. He leaned toward the dashboard and tried to see what happened when they rang the bell, but Mrs. Hartounian's hibiscus bush obscured his view of the front door. The same kids walked away moments later, rowdy with satisfaction as they rooted through their bags. Ross watched as they vanished into the night, taking with them booty from his father.

There were times as a child when some petty deprivation—a toy or a favor he'd been denied—had made Ross red-faced, contorted with tears, and he felt a phantom of that wanting now, stark and inconsolable. He swallowed hard, gripped the wheel.

And then a plan lit him from inside.

Ross reached around and grabbed one of the barber drapes he'd tossed into the backseat. He spread the fabric across his lap, guessed at its center, and jabbed two ragged holes with his car key. After cloaking himself beneath the disguise, he examined it in the rearview mirror. If he didn't move his head too much, the eyeholes worked, and his view of the world was unobstructed.

As he stepped onto the sidewalk, the drape fanned behind him like ectoplasm. Breath warmed the cotton that covered his face. Because he wore running shoes, his footsteps were muffled against the pavement, air moving beneath his feet. He felt like himself, but ethereal, freed from the laws of propriety and physics, as if he were dreaming himself toward home.

A warm Santa Ana gusted through the city, shook the trees and electrified the air. Every now and then he had to grip the drape from inside and brace it against the gusts of wind. He took a moment to compose himself beside Mrs. Hartounian's hibiscus bush. Mitsy, the arthritic, white-faced cocker spaniel that Mrs. Hartounian never bothered to lock in her yard or keep on a leash, lay on the grass like a dusty throw rug. She opened her eyes when she sensed Ross's presence, then grunted once before she closed them.

A mother dressed as Vampira walked past, dragging a tiny
hobo behind her. Thanks to wrinkled clothes and a face
smudged with charcoal, the child gave an excellent impression
of indigence and filth. Ross chirped a hi to assure them he was
harmless, that he had some reason for loitering. Vampira
smiled and led the hobo up his father's walk, long black hair
swaying behind her. Peering around the bush, Ross could see
the colonial house he'd once lived in, as immense and stately
as an ocean liner. The hedges were trimmed, the shutters
freshly painted. Apparently, dispossessing a son hadn't put a
dent in his father's life, or at least in his home. Ross realized
then that he'd hoped to see some evidence of his father's regret, some blow to pride of ownership: the paint peeling, the
shutters unhinged. Instead, framed within the wide bay window, the living room, which had never seemed particularly
inviting to Ross when he was a child, glowed now with lamplight, an inaccessible sanctuary, every pillow within it plumped,
the mahogany furniture sturdy and burnished.

Mr. Gold opened the door, wearing a polyester safari suit
that those less familiar with his wardrobe might have mistaken
for a costume. Only the rifle and pith helmet were missing. He
took a moment to beam at the boy and pat his head, finally
pouring chocolate bars from a crystal bowl. The hobo held up
a gaping paper sack and gazed into his benefactor's face. Ross
eyed the waterfall of chocolate and, once the boy and his
mother had left, wafted toward his father's house.

At the lip of his father's walkway, he met a trio of unsuper-
vised boys who were dressed as Bat-, Spider-, and Superman.
After scrutinizing him from behind their masks, they accepted
him into their midst; Ross was just another stranger begging
for sweets. When the four of them reached the porch, Ross

took it upon himself to ring the doorbell, something he'd never done in the past when he'd felt entitled to use his key. The doorbell chimed three mellow notes, prelude to countless welcomings he used to hear from inside the house. The pack of trick-or-treaters paused, shifting their weight on the flagstone porch.

Although it had been a year since he'd actually seen his father, Ross thought he saw him everywhere. Almost once a week, if the cast of light and the distance conspired, some balding, bespectacled old man tripped the alarm of recognition. Ross would catch his mistake before he called out and waved to the stranger, but the sound of "Dad?" would stick in his throat.

What baffled Ross most was how their fight had started. They'd been sitting in his father's sunny kitchen, discussing one of Mr. Gold's recent parking tickets; he parked his Regal wherever he pleased. His father's refusal to pay the fine wasn't surprising—he'd always been a stubborn man, slow to admit he'd been in the wrong—but as he talked to Ross about the ticket his age-spotted hands began to tremble and his brown eyes, magnified by horn-rimmed glasses, clouded with rage. It was as if every injustice, every tribulation of his seventy years had been written down on a pink slip of paper and slapped on his windshield for all the world to see. Ross sat back, thinking it best to let his father fume. "Bet you wouldn't pay it," his father snapped, "if you were me. You probably couldn't afford to on that income of yours."

"Just a minute," Ross insisted, so stunned by his father's remark that he wasn't aware his voice had risen. "I make a decent living cutting hair." Day after day, men marveled at a flawless part, or the symmetry of bristling sideburns. He refused to let his father's insult slide. But the second Ross protested, Mr. Gold had grabbed his son's shirt, his face clenched and alien with effort. "Don't you ever raise your voice at me!" he'd yelled. "Don't forget that I'm your father. Now get the hell out and don't come back."

Taller and stronger than his father, Ross could easily have fought back or wrenched himself free, but he let himself be shoved toward the door. Once outside, he turned on the landing. He expected to see his father purged of anger, hands in his pockets, embarrassed by his flaring temper and ready to make amends. Instead his father was slamming the door. Ross reached out and stopped it from closing, but Mr. Gold heaved against it with his shoulder.

"This is crazy," said Ross, pushing back from the other side.

"I'm not as crazy as you think."

"Not you. This. Over parking tickets." The door began to creak with pressure, the brittle sound of wood giving way.

"I'm old," said his father, breathing hard. "I'm an old man and I can do whatever the hell I want. I don't have to answer to anyone. Not anymore I don't. And that includes you."

His father's voice, enraged and frail, caused the fight to drain from Ross's body. The whole house rattled when the door hit the jamb, the lock clicking, definitive.

Standing among a bunch of kids, Ross faced the door through which he'd been ejected; it was painted green with a small brass knocker, like the entrance to hundreds of other homes. And just as that door began to swing open, an updraft ballooned within the drape and threatened to send it flying away. Ross caught it and pulled it taut. He tugged on the cotton and angled his head, but one crooked eyehole wouldn't straighten out and a circle of Ross's cheek was exposed. He gazed at his father with the other eye. Gaunt and unsteady on his feet, Mr. Gold nevertheless managed to gawk at his visitors with great theatricality, arching his unruly white eyebrows, his mouth an "O" of surprise. As if on cue, the kids crooned a chorus of "Trick or treat!" Ross piped in a little too late. He'd intended to keep quiet, but that Halloween cry was a deep-seated reflex. He hoped his father hadn't recognized his voice, deeper and yet more eager than the others. When Mr. Gold turned to face him, Ross noticed, as though for the first time, the freckled scalp, the tired eyes, and patches of stubble the razor had missed—a glimpse of his future face in his father's.

"My, my," said Mr. Gold, "you're a big one."

Before Ross could think of a response, the superheroes thrust out their bags, reminding Mr. Gold of his obligation. While his father went to retrieve the crystal bowl from a table in the foyer, Ross adjusted his eyeholes and sidled closer to the door. The grandfather clock ticked in a corner. The checkered floor of the foyer was spotless, and Ross figured his father still employed the maid who'd worked at the house since his mother's death. His father's solitude was muted by money; Ross gazed at the comforts from which he'd been banished. Had his comparative poverty embarrassed his father? Maybe so, but wasn't Ross a person who paid his bills, kept his appointments, washed his Chevy Nova once a month? *I'm a responsible adult,* he assured himself, tugging the costume taut.

The hobo must have absconded with all the chocolate because the crystal bowl now brimmed with Bit-O-Honey, a candy Ross might never have recalled had he not seen it again this evening. His father dumped fistfuls of the stuff into bag after bag—those delectable rectangles pelting the paper!—until he came to Ross. The sight of his father reaching toward him caused Ross's arms to levitate. The drape slid down to the crook of his elbows and he found himself forming a cup with his palms. He hoped his hairy forearms and broad hands wouldn't give him away. "Where's your bag?" his father asked, the Bit-O-Honeys poised in midair.

Ross continued to stand there, a pillar of cotton rippling in the wind. The kids stared up at the two adults and waited for something to happen. "Hey, look!" Superman shouted when Mitsy hobbled through his legs and into Mr. Gold's house. She stopped to sneeze in the middle of the foyer, the tags on her collar tinkling like wind chimes, then limped into the living room. Mr. Gold turned in pursuit, his hearing aid squealing from the sudden motion. The door blew shut, groaning on its hinges, but Ross reached out and stopped it from closing.

He spun around and faced the kids. "You can go now."

"Who died and made you king?" said Batman.

"Yeah," said Spiderman.

"This is my house," said Ross.

"Oh, sure," said Superman.

Ross pointed into the night. "Get off my property." How nostalgic to invoke that threat, just like he had as a boy.

"Asshole," one of them mumbled.

Ross lunged. Superheroes leapt off the landing and scattered across the front lawn, epithets trailing in their wake.

After the kids had disappeared, Ross scanned the street in both directions. Leaves rattled in the warm, insistent wind, and a few trick-or-treaters laughed in the distance. He slipped through the door as smoothly as vapor. He could hardly believe what he was doing, but now that he haunted his father's house, he had to be stealthy and insubstantial; one clumsy move and he might get arrested, or scare his father half to death. He padded past the archway that led to the living room and saw his father bending over Mitsy. Feedback still shrieked from the hearing aid. Frightened by the noise, Mitsy cowered against the sofa. When Mr. Gold reached out to touch her, she raised her face and bayed, her howl milder and more forlorn than any Ross had ever heard. Mr. Gold finally quieted the hearing aid, but he continued to stroke the spaniel's ears and tried to calm her by talking nonsense. "Crazy pooch, sneaky little goof." Ross could hear the faint, absurd endearments as he glided up the stairs of the house where he was born. He recalled precisely which steps creaked—how intimate he was with this house, would always be—and skipped them with ease.

Once he reached the second-story landing, he held onto the banister and stared into the room below, trying to stay as calm and inconspicuous as possible. Mr. Gold carried Mitsy into the foyer and set her down. "Shoo," he said, holding open the door. As soon as the dog hobbled off, Mr. Gold locked the front door and switched off the porch light, giving up on Halloween early. Hovering above his father, Ross remembered hearing how the dead, before they transcend to another plane, peer down from the heights of the life they once lived and view it with new detachment. Mr. Gold gathered up packages of candy, sighing deeply now and then, his pate shining beneath the chandelier. Ross had wanted to believe his father was a monster, mean to everyone he met, but Mr. Gold had spent the night tending to children and a neighbor's ancient dog.

Only after his father carried the leftover candy into the kitchen did Ross become aware of a woman's voice emanating from the master bedroom down the hall. Although he couldn't make out what the woman was saying, she seemed to be making promises. *So this has been his secret,* thought Ross: a lover sprawled on the king-size bed, rehearsing invitations to kiss and caress her. Perhaps his father had been afraid all along that Ross would find out he kept a woman—by the sound of her, young and practiced in seduction. Maybe his girlfriend, clearing a path to Mr. Gold's money, had encouraged him to cut off contact with Ross. Or maybe she'd convinced his father to turn his back because Ross was gay, appalled that Mr. Gold had taken his sexuality in stride. These possibilities, only a few among the dozens he'd ruminated over for the past year— *Maybe if I hadn't raised my voice, had visited him more often, had been another kind of son*—suddenly seemed plausible. He drifted toward the master bedroom, a migration of pure curiosity, certain he was close to an answer at last.

His eyes adjusted to the dark hallway. Leather-bound classics lined a shelf. A print of a mallard gleamed under glass. When he heard a sudden creaking from the stairwell—could it be his father climbing the stairs?—Ross dashed into his old room. It surprised him to find the door wide open; he would have guessed that his father kept it closed. He pressed against the bedroom wall, his muscles tense, his breathing ragged. When the creaking subsided—the house must have been settling—so did his panic. Ross fluffed his costume and walked around the room. His desk and bureau, a high school pennant tacked to the wall—"Go Rovers!"—had remained unchanged for nearly fifteen years. The smell of wood polish and mothballs was stronger than he remembered. Cold, preserving moonlight fell through the windows and made his room seem like a diorama, each artifact in its place. Ross touched the lampshade, the bedspread, the chair, as separate from his boyhood as he was from his father.

The woman's distant, sultry voice roused him from his

reverie. Once he was certain there was no one in the hall, he tiptoed out of his room, determined to finish his mission. He crept beside the door to the master bedroom and tried to figure out how he could peek inside without being seen. The drape might help him blend into the walls of the hallway. Or else his father's girlfriend, in the middle of her monologue, would glimpse a ghost in the doorway and scream. Either way, he needed to see this woman through his own two eyeholes, and the fact that he might made his mouth go dry. "I've got what you've been waiting for," she murmured. "Here it comes, ready or not." Then came the chords of "We've Only Just Begun." The instant Ross understood his mistake, an electric piano glissandoed. He stepped into the moonlit room and there was the radio on his father's nightstand. "Hey, out there," said the DJ. "This is Lila O'Day bringing you *Sounds in the Night.*"

Ross had grown hot beneath his costume. He yanked off the drape—the drag of fabric made his short brown hair crackle with static—and bunched it under his arm. Here was the room where his father came to brood. Without farewell or explanation, Mr. Gold would rise from the dinner table before he'd finished a meal, or from the couch before the six o'clock news had ended. Once he began to climb the stairs, no entreaty could bring him back. Sometimes he disappeared when company was visiting, the guests too shy or polite to ask Mrs. Gold if anything was wrong. Ross and his mother knew to let him go, knew that he'd return an hour or two later, purged by silence and isolation. Since Ross could never fathom the reasons behind these flights into privacy, he'd wondered instead if his father paced the floor, or stared through the window, or slumped on the edge of the bed. Only as a small child was Ross granted the privilege of entering the master bedroom unannounced;

when frightened by the leafy people who appeared in the trees outside his bedroom window, he'd barge into his parents' room, finding rest in the valley between their bodies.

Even in the gloom, Ross saw the pink of several parking tickets piled atop the desk in the corner. Drawn closer, he sat in the desk chair, its claw feet gripping the floor. His father kept the tickets weighted down by the Lucite picture cube his mother had bought shortly before her death. Cancer had stripped Mrs. Gold of her flesh, but gave new life to her sentiment; she intended to fill each side of the cube with snapshots of friends and relatives, though she'd quickly grown too sick. His father hadn't bothered to replace the photographs of models that came in the cube: frisky kids, loving couples, and spry old folks. Bland and random examples of family.

Ross couldn't resist thumbing through the unpaid tickets. He squinted at the range of violations—from double parking to an expired meter. His father had accumulated over a dozen fines. How long before they clamped a Denver boot onto his car? Ross carefully began replacing the tickets just as he'd found them, as if he'd never set foot inside the house. Tonight, his erasure was within his own power, not his father's.

Hunched over the desk, his back to the door, Ross suddenly stopped what he was doing, alert to a shift in the atmosphere. He spun around and faced his father. Wearing a bathrobe and a pair of fleecy slippers, Mr. Gold was framed in the doorway. His knee joints cracked as he walked toward his son. His legs, the hair grown sparse with age, were white as bone. Ross held his breath and drew back toward the desk, gripping the picture cube until its edges dug into his palm. Mr. Gold hadn't switched on the bedroom light; his face was in shadow and it was impossible to tell whether he was approaching with as-

tonishment or rage or tenderness. Ross searched the furthest
reaches of his imagination for a legitimate excuse to be sitting
in his father's bedroom, uninvited, in the middle of the night.
There was no excuse, only the obdurate need to see him. "I'm
sorry," he was about to say aloud, but he'd said it in a letter to
no avail, and there seemed no point in saying it again. When
his father walked through a stripe of moonlight, Ross saw that
his face held neither wonderment nor animosity nor love. Except for the effort of moving forward, he bore no expression
whatsoever. Mr. Gold stared through his son. He carried his bifocals and hearing aid in one hand, and a glass of effervescing
liquid in the other. The closer he came, the louder the sound of
hissing bubbles. It seemed an act of divine intervention when
Mr. Gold turned before he reached the desk, a few yards away
from his gaping boy. He moved to his side of the bed and set
his belongings on the nightstand. Ross watched him pluck out
his dentures and drop them into the glass. Teeth touched bottom with a subaquatic clink. They left behind a mouthful of
emptiness, like something unsaid, when Mr. Gold yawned.

Having shed his senses, Mr. Gold was unable to see or hear
the intruder huddled in the far corner of the room. He removed his bathrobe, nude underneath. Flesh sagged from his
shoulders and hips. A shock of pale hair covered his groin. Mr.
Gold laid the robe at the foot of the bed and pulled back the
blanket. Oblivious to the news issuing from the radio—a report on the usual Halloween pranks and hooliganism—Ross's
father climbed into bed and closed his eyes, a remote, dis-
mantled man.

Once the immediate danger of being caught had passed,
Ross realized he was trembling. Blood banged in his temples.
It took him a while to feel his hands and feet, to wrench him-

self out of the chair. Hugging the bundled drape to his stomach, he moved through the bedroom in slow motion, the floorboards creaking with every step. All the while he kept an eye on his father to make sure he didn't stir. Mr. Gold began to snore, drifting deeper and deeper into enviable forgetfulness.

Ross had reached the bedroom door when his father asked a question. The words were airy and unintelligible, more like the wind than the voice of a man. His eyes fluttered but didn't open. His arms twitched briefly, then stilled at his sides. The old man looked so slack in the bed, he spoke in such a plaintive tone, that Ross couldn't help but answer. "Yes," he said, though he wasn't sure to what he'd assented. Mr. Gold suddenly heaved himself up and rolled onto his stomach.

Ross flew down the staircase and through the foyer, nearly slipping on the polished tile. The front door was a riddle of brass latches and stubborn deadbolts. When the door finally opened, brittle leaves blew over the threshold and scratched across the checkered floor. Ross didn't stop to close the door behind him. Not until he'd raced down the flagstone path and leapt into his Chevy, not until he'd stepped on the gas and lurched from the curb, did he dare to look back. In the rearview mirror, his old house hurtled into the night at twenty, twenty-five miles per hour, the roof and windows and clapboard walls vanishing like an apparition.

The outlandishness of what he had done began to fade on the drive back to his apartment. Breaking and entering seemed almost ordinary compared to the trees festooned with toilet paper streamers, a fishpond frothing over with soapsuds, or a headless man filling his tank at a Standard station.

It wasn't until he arrived home that he found the Lucite cube. It lay in the folds of his crumpled costume. He must have run off with it gripped in his fist. The missing picture cube, the unlocked door, the leaves strewn across the foyer—he worried that his father might report the break-in to the police. But who could make sense of such a crime? It was a mystery Mr. Gold would have to live with.

The next day, Ross told a few friends that he'd finally seen his father in the flesh, though he downplayed the fantastic circumstances surrounding their reunion. When pressed for details, Ross told them he was "all talked out" about his father, weary of guesses and speculation.

The picture cube found a prominent place on his counter at the shop, next to a tin of talcum powder and a bottle of styling gel. Sometimes a client asked who the people were. Ross would turn off his electric clippers and brush stray hairs from the customer's neck. He'd pick up the cube—it weighed next to nothing—and turn it in his hand. A stranger gazed from every side.

hunters and
gatherers

Rick had been searching for the Pillings' address for over twenty minutes, and the hungrier he became, the harder it was to concentrate on the dimly lit street signs, the six-digit numbers stenciled on curbs. Westgate Village was a planned community an hour away from the downtown loft where Rick lived, its street names a variation on the same bucolic phrase: Valley Vista Circle, Village Road, Valley View Court. Each one-story ranch house looked nearly the same except for the color of its garage door, and Rick, who'd skipped lunch, began to wonder if the entire suburb was a hunger-induced hallucination. Jerry Pilling, giddy as a kid at the prospect of throwing a party, had given Rick hasty directions over the phone so many weeks ago that Rick now had a hard time deciphering his own scrawl. He pulled over to the curb, squinted at what he'd written on a scrap of paper, and tried to retrace his turns. All the while, digestive juices sluiced through his stomach and a dull ache came and went.

Rick was about to give up and head for a phone booth when a Mustang crept past, the driver peering this way and that, on the prowl for an address. Jerry had described the party as a chance for his wife, Meg, to meet a group of his gay friends, and after much wrangling she'd finally agreed, but only on the condition that she could invite her hairdresser, the one "avowed" homosexual she knew. Rick had a hunch that the man driving the Mustang was Mrs. Pilling's hairdresser—the skin of his face was shiny and taut, his silver hair moussed—and decided to follow him. "Avowed" had about it a quaint, anachronistic ring, and Rick pictured a dandy in an ascot, hand raised as he swore some sort of oath. Sure enough, the Mustang pulled up to the right address within minutes. A house with double doors and deep eaves, it sat at the end of a cul-de-sac. "Pilling" was chiseled on a wooden sign, the front lawn glowing greenly in the dusk.

Rick had met Jerry Pilling on a midnight flight from New York to Los Angeles. Returning home from his one-man show at a SoHo gallery, Rick was solvent and optimistic for the first time in a year. Seatmates in the back of the plane, the two of them struck up a conversation, or rather, Rick listened across the dark heartlands of America as tiny bottles of Smirnoff's accumulated on Jerry's tray table. "Meg and I are Mormons," Jerry told him, shaking the last drops of alcohol into his plastic tumbler, "so we aren't allowed to drink. But I bend the rules depending on the altitude." He touched Rick's arm and his breath, as pungent as jet fuel, sterilized the air between them.

"I'm terrified of flying." This was the first of Jerry's confessions; soon they came with escalating candor, the consonants softened by booze. "Do you know any Mormons?" asked Jerry. "Personally, I mean."

"Only impersonally." Rick laughed.

"Well, take it from me, not all of us are polygamists who bathe in our holy undergarments. There's lots of ways to be a Mormon; at least, that's the way *I* see it."

"There's a Mormon guy at my gym," ventured Rick, "who wears the garments under his workout clothes, even in summer."

"Or proselytize on our bicycles."

"I'm sorry?"

"Not all of us proselytize on our bicycles."

Rick pictured Jerry wobbling on a Schwinn.

"Listen," said Jerry, giving Rick a let's-lay-our-cards-on-the-tray-table look. "Are you by any chance . . . I don't mean to be presumptuous, so forgive me if I'm wrong, but you haven't said anything about a wife, and I was wondering if you're . . ."

"Gay?"

"I knew it!" blurted Jerry, slapping his armrest. "I have a sick sense—sixth sense—about these things. I am, too!"

To Rick's way of thinking, Jerry was unduly excited by this coincidence, as if he'd discovered they had the same mother. Still, he found something intriguing about the portly, candid stranger beside him. He eyed Jerry's wedding ring and, with no prompting whatsoever, Jerry launched into the story of his marriage. "I only recently told Meg that I fooled around with men in college. Groping a house brother, that sort of thing." This piqued Rick's interest and he had to steer Jerry back to the subject when, trying to recall the name of his fraternity, he was sidetracked into a muddled pronunciation of Greek letters. "The point," continued Jerry, "is that I wanted to write off my college flings as trial and error, youthful confusion. But after six children and twenty years of marriage, I couldn't ignore my thing for guys. College men especially. Studious types. Blond. With glasses." Jerry sighed. "The more I tried to pray it away, the stronger it got."

The plane hit a patch of turbulence over Kansas. Snug in his seat and buffered by vodka, Jerry didn't seem to notice. Passengers shifted beneath their blankets. A baby bawled in the forward cabin. "We counseled with the church elders, Meg and me, and they thought that male companionship—strictly platonic, of course—would help me 'scratch the itch,' as they put it. So we decided to stay married and faithful, and I'm going to make some homosexual friends." Jerry brightened. "We'll have to have you over for dinner."

"The church *wants* you to have gay friends?"

"Hey," said Jerry, shifting in his seat. "They didn't say homosexual or not. But 'male companionship' is open to interpretation, don't you think?" He stirred his drink with an index finger, then sucked his finger and took a swig. "According to the church, if me and Meg get divorced, old Jerry here wanders around heaven for time immemorial, a soul without a family."

It was delicate: Rick didn't want to challenge Jerry's religious beliefs, but he found this punishment cruel and unusual, not to mention superstitious. "Do you really believe that's what would happen?"

"The idea scares me whether I believe in it or not. An outcast even after I'm dead. Lifelong bonds coming to nothing. Estranged from my very own kids." He chewed an ice cube and shivered. "I joined Affirmation, a group of gay Mormons, and they say the church is run by humans, and humans don't know everything there is to know about the Creator's plan; only one judgment matters in the end, and at least He'll know what made me tick and how I tried to do what's right. But Rick," said Jerry, leaning close, "here's where I part company with the folks at Affirmation: they're skeptical about a man staying married."

"You mean, about a gay man staying married?"

"Isn't that what I said? Anyway, living in a family makes me happy. My kids are turning into people I like. You should see the little ones swamp me when I walk through the door. Chalk it up to my having been an only child, but even when they're fighting and crying, the chaos is kind of cozy, you know?"

"What about your wife?"

"I'd tried to tell her when we were dating, but she'd shush me and say the past didn't matter. It probably didn't occur to her I was messing with men. She wanted a husband and I wanted to be normal; in that respect we were meant for each other. And here I am." Jerry looked around, then whispered, "I'm the only man Meg has ever slept with. And let me tell you, I've never pretended. I've always loved her and I always will. In the bedroom, too. Love must count for something, right?"

"It should," said Rick. He wished that Eric, the man he had lived with, was still alive and waiting at home. "If it were up to me," he told Jerry, "love would stop trains and change the weather."

The seat belt signs were turned off and a low electronic bell rang throughout the cabin. "Sorry if I talked your ear off," said Jerry. "I ought to keep my big mouth shut. But keeping quiet wears me out a lot more than talking." His head lolled toward the oval window. Rick leaned forward and gazed out, too. Beads of condensation gathered on the glass. Dawn-tinted fields and rooftops and roads were visible through thinning clouds.

The double doors swung open and there stood Mrs. Pilling, her tight auburn curls a miracle of modern cosmetology. She glanced back and forth between Rick and her hairdresser, smiling nervously. "Did you and Oscar come together?" she asked. Perhaps she assumed that Rick and Oscar had crossed paths in the small province of their "lifestyle." Rick felt a pang of sympathy for Meg; *She's trying to hold up the walls,* he thought, *just like the rest of us.* Dressed in slinky blue culottes, eyelids dusted with matching shadow, Meg appeared every inch the camera-ready hostess; the only thing missing, lamented Rick, was a platter of canapés. He felt certain her stylish outfit was meant to show her husband's unconventional friends that she was a woman with flair, not the stodgy, narrow-minded matron they might have expected.

"It's serendipity," Oscar told her, handing over a pungent bouquet. "We met tonight on this very doorstep."

"Oscar treats me like a queen," said Meg, plunging her powdered nose into the flowers.

Jerry Pilling darted out the door. "Gentlemen," he bellowed, "welcome to the hinterlands!" His hail voice and vise-like handshake were far more manly than Rick remembered. Dressed in loose black linen, Oscar rippled as Jerry pumped his hand. "Meg's raved about you," he told Oscar. "Says you're the only man who can give her hair volume."

"Noblesse oblige," said Oscar. He turned toward Mrs. Pilling. "Meg, dear, you'd better get that nosegay into some water."

Rick and Oscar followed the Pillings into a spacious living

room, as ornate, thought Rick, as a rococo salon. Overstuffed sofas and chairs were covered in plaids and herringbones and stripes. One wall was an archive of framed family photographs. Jerry and Meg pointed to the pictures and boasted about their kids in unison—a long, overlapping roll call—and it sounded to Rick as if they'd given birth to a happy hive, several more than the half-dozen children Jerry'd mentioned on the plane. Snapshots in which the whole family posed together had the voluminous look of class pictures. Rick imagined the Pillings' grocery cart loaded to the brim with potato chip bags, Cheerios boxes as big as luggage, six-packs of soda, gallons of milk. While the Pillings, as verbose as docents, led him along the wall, Rick searched every tabletop for a bowl of peanuts or a wedge of cheese, finding instead an endless array of ceramic animals, dried flowers, and colorful blown-glass clowns. The clowns looked as though they were molded out of hard candy, and Rick could almost taste their antic faces.

"Where *is* your brood?" asked Oscar.

"Simon's at debating. Mandy's at ballet. The rest of the kids have already eaten. They're in their rooms doing who knows what." Jerry nodded toward a hallway that burrowed deep into one wing of the house. Light seeped from beneath its row of doors.

"I'll check on the kids," said Meg.

"How 'bout I show you the grounds," said Jerry, slapping them both on the back.

The yard was a vast expanse of concrete, a kidney-shaped swimming pool in the center. Lit from within, the pool threw woozy refractions onto the surrounding cinder-block walls. Pool toys bobbed atop the water like flotsam from a shipwreck. An inflatable shark, bleached by the sun, floated belly-up. Jerry bent down at the edge of the pool and fiddled with the water filter, which made a shrill sucking noise; from behind, it looked as if he were trying to drink the pool through a straw. Blood sugar plummeting, Rick wondered if it would be impolite to ask for a Coke, or whether he should wait until something was offered. He scolded himself for being a recluse; if he got out of the studio more often, he might know how to behave in these situations.

The sliding glass doors rumbled open and Meg ushered the remaining guests into the warm night. Mitchell Coply was Jerry's dentist. A man in his early forties, he had the slim, diminutive build of a schoolboy. A lock of hair sprang onto his forehead no matter how often he brushed it away. His puckish appearance was contradicted by tired, melancholy eyes behind his gold-rimmed glasses. During the round of introductions, Mitchell was soft-spoken and shy about eye contact, the kind of man incapable of concealing his sadness. Jan Kirby was an agent who worked with Jerry at a real estate office that specialized in new housing developments throughout the San Fernando Valley. Tall and broad-shouldered, Jan wore a pin-striped pants suit and running shoes. After meeting the other guests, she stood perilously close to the edge of the pool and faced the deep end, hands on her hips. Lit from below by the pool light, she looked to Rick like a deity about to part, or walk across, the water. "After dessert," she said in her husky voice, "let's go skinny-dipping." It took everyone a second to realize she was joking. Mrs. Pilling wagged a finger at Jan—naughty, naughty—and gave a fair imitation of laughter.

By the time the guests reassembled indoors to see the Pillings' remodeled kitchen, Rick was actively praying for snack food. The thought of salty pretzels possessed him, though he'd have happily settled for Triscuits, Cheese Nips, anything with weight and flavor. Meg Pilling ran her manicured hand across the width of a new refrigerator, like one of those models who stroke appliances on game shows. The built-in icemaker suddenly dumped a few chiming ice cubes into a tumbler. Mitchell nodded thoughtfully. Oscar applauded and said, "Brava!" Jan asked if the refrigerator could heel or play dead. Only after the demonstration did Rick notice the absence of cooking odors. The windows of the double ovens were dark, the granite countertops barren. Copper pots hung above the electric range in descending size, mere decoration. Rick tried to fight his hangdog expression; hadn't Jerry said there'd be dinner?

"Folks," announced Jerry, after corralling everyone into the living room. "Have a seat. The wife and I have a little surprise." The four guests squeezed among an avalanche of tasseled pillows, sinking side by side into the couch. "Honey," Jerry said to Meg, "you've got the floor."

Meg Pilling walked to the center of the room. She taught at Westgate Elementary, which explained her exemplary posture and the lilting, patient cadence of her voice. Rick had no trouble envisioning a troupe of mesmerized second-graders following her every order. He wondered if she was about to ask them to make their dinner out of paste and construction paper.

Meg cleared her throat and gazed into the upturned faces of her guests. "Jerry and I wanted to do something fun and unusual, so we've planned a really outlandish night." She grinned and shot a look at her husband. Jerry beamed back. "I bet you're all just itching to know what it is." As if on cue, everyone mumbled and shifted about. "Well . . .," she said, milking the suspense, "we're going to give you each five dollars and let you go to the store on your own—there are several excellent supermarkets in the area—so you can buy something to fix for a potluck!"

No one stirred or spoke. Rick wasn't sure he'd heard her correctly.

"We have all the cooking utensils you'll need," said Meg. "And that brand-new kitchen is just sitting there, waiting! The only rules are that you don't go over your five-dollar limit, and that you're back here within half an hour."

"Do we have to actually cook what we buy?" asked Mitchell. The idea of culinary effort seemed to depress him. "Can't we buy something frozen or from the deli section?"

Meg's smile wavered. Through the crack in her composure, Rick thought he glimpsed a hint of misery. "Now that wouldn't be very creative, would it?" She looked at her husband as if to say, *You've got to prod some people into the party spirit.*

"I get it," rasped Jan. "Hunters and gatherers!"

"How primitive," said Oscar.

"I used to love scavenger hunts," said Mitchell. "Of course, those were the days when a kid could knock on a stranger's door without being molested or kidnapped." He pushed his glasses up the bridge of his nose.

"Well," said Meg, reviving her smile, "you're safe in Westgate."

"She's absolutely right," said Jerry. "If you're not back in half an hour, we'll file a report with the Bureau of Missing Persons." He removed a wallet from his back pocket and dealt out five-dollar bills. Peering up from a sitting position, reaching for what amounted to his allowance, Rick had to admit that, fiscally speaking, Jerry fit the paternal role, confident and ceremonious as he handled money.

"Largesse!" exclaimed Oscar. He took his five and winked at Rick.

"I ironed them," said Meg, to explain the crisp, unblemished bills. "Are there any more questions?"

Rick was going to ask the Pillings to give him explicit directions back to the house so he wouldn't get lost again, but he was nearly moved to tears by the thought that he could not only buy food for the potluck, but also something to eat right away, even before he got to the cash register. He was first to rise to his feet, a move which, considering the plush upholstery, took some leverage. The others straggled after him, sharing baffled glances. Meg and Jerry each grabbed a knob of the double doors and swung them open. "I wish I had a starting gun," said Jerry.

Mitchell paused in the doorway and asked, "Aren't you coming, too?"

From the way the Pillings looked at each other, it was clear this possibility hadn't crossed their minds. "We'll keep the home fires burning," said Jerry.

"Your best bet is to head back to the freeway exit," said Meg. "Toward the commercial district. You can't miss it." She watched her guests scatter across the front lawn, trudging toward their cars.

"Just look for signs of life," yelled Jerry.

Once inside his car, Rick noticed Jan in a Mercedes parked across the street, her face lit by the glow of a cigarette lighter, cheeks imploding as she took the first drag. Parked behind her, Mitchell furrowed his brow and squinted at a road map, disappearing within its folds. Oscar barreled by in his Mustang, shrugging at Rick and honking his horn. Jerry and Meg stood beside each other in the wide bright doorway of their sprawling home. They waved at Rick as he revved his engine, one fluttering arm per spouse.

*　　*　　*

Anyone who saw the Pillings in their doorway that night would probably take their happiness and compatibility for granted. Rick wondered what, if anything, Jan and Oscar and Mitchell knew about the couple's compromised marriage. He wouldn't have been surprised to learn that Meg and Jerry had let their secrets slip; it's easy, thought Rick, to confide in someone you see at work, or to someone who runs his fingers through your hair, or probes your open mouth.

As he pulled away from the curb, he couldn't help but marvel at the Pillings' elaborate domesticity: offspring, swimming pool, blown-glass clowns. While touring their home, he had sensed that Meg and Jerry meant to impress each other more than their visitors: *See what we have. See what we've done. Our life together is no illusion, no mistake.*

Since Oscar seemed to know where he was going, Rick tried to catch up with the Mustang's taillights, but they shot away like comets near a street named Valley Court. Checking his rearview mirror for Mitchell and Jan, he saw nothing but the empty road behind him. Once again, Rick found himself navigating the maze of Westgate, its lawns trimmed, its houses all alike. He aimed his car toward a concentration of hazy light, a distant promise of people and commerce.

It had been so long since Rick had cooked a meal, he was worried he'd forgotten how. Working in his studio till dinnertime, light-headed from paint fumes, he'd usually stand before the open refrigerator and nibble at scraps of food, or jump into his car and head for Casa Carnitas, the local taco stand. Dinners had been different when Eric was alive. The two of them sometimes dedicated entire nights to the alchemy of cooking;

the raw becoming tender, the cold becoming hot. Chopping and stirring and sautéing not only took time but seemed to prolong it, the minutes enriched with their arguments and gossip. When their studio grew warm and fragrant with sauces and roasts, Rick found himself believing that Eric might never succumb to the virus. Not if he could be tempted by food. Not if he gained weight.

"I wouldn't be so worried if I could put on a few pounds," Eric told him one night, peering down at himself as if over the edge of a cliff. The weaker Eric's appetite, the more time he and Rick spent planning and preparing meals. They began to visit farmers' markets, carnicerias, bakeries. At a restaurant supply store near Chinatown, they bought a garlic press, a set of wire whisks, and what they decided was their most frivolous purchase to date: a lemon zester. Although he often couldn't finish a meal, Eric insisted that cooking gave him pleasure, distracted him from the neuropathy that numbed his lips and hands and feet. They had sex less often now that Eric was home all day, groggy from medication, and Rick suspected that their libido, rerouted, had given birth to lavish repasts.

In the early evenings, Rick cleaned his brushes, climbed the stairs to the sleeping loft, and crawled into bed beside Eric. The mattress lay on the floor, surrounded by issues of *Art in America*, bottles of AZT, and crumpled clothes. Rick would reach beneath Eric's sweatshirt and rub his back while they watched cooking shows on television, both of them soothed by the warmth and give of skin. On Channel 13, Madeleine Duprey might fricassee a game hen or make a sumptuous ratatouille, rolling her R's with such panache, they began to doubt she was really French. Then there was Our Man Masami, a chef who dismembered vegetables with a glinting cleaver and laughed a high, delirious laugh as he tossed them into a hissing wok. Rick and Eric took notes while they watched, salivating. They cheered and grumbled like football fans, shouting comments like "Needs something crunchy!" or "Too much cumin!"

Over time, however, it was Rick who grew padded with fat, his trousers tight around the waist, while Eric, whittled by the blade of AIDS, could barely bring himself to eat.

Alarmed by Eric's weight loss, Dr. Santos started him on a regimen of Oxandrin tablets, steroid injections, and cans of a rich nutritional drink. His weight finally stabilized, but his already pale skin continued to grow translucent. Rick began to notice thin blue veins beneath Eric's temples, wrists, and groin, a glimpse into the tributaries, the secret depths of his lover's flesh. Still, Rick held on to the hope that he was only imagining Eric's fragility, making it into something more ominous than it really was. Until one Sunday at the farmers' market.

They were walking back to their car, both of them carrying bags of fresh food. Eric had been in good spirits that morning, eager for an outing. Enormous clouds raced overhead, wind strafing the city streets. Taking a shortcut, they turned down an alley, and a sudden gust funneled toward them. Eric's jacket blew open, the red lining as bright as blood, and he toppled backward, landing on his side, apples and onions spilling from the bags. Sprawled on the asphalt, Eric couldn't move his arm, and Rick knelt down to cradle his head. "Is this happening?" Eric asked. An eerie calm tempered his voice, as if he'd observed, from far away, the fall of some frail, unlucky stranger.

In the emergency room, while Eric was being X-rayed, Rick told the attending physician that Eric must have tripped on a crack in the asphalt and lost his footing. But later, sitting alone in the waiting room, he couldn't stop repeating to himself, *A gust of wind knocked Eric over.*

AZT, it turned out, had made his bones brittle, and so Dr. Santos discontinued Eric's antiretrovirals until his fractured arm had time to heal. This led to complications that worsened Eric's weight loss. The most dire was an inability to absorb nutrients. Now and then he managed sips of broth, cubes of Jell-O, diluted juice, but nothing he ate or drank sustained him. Eric was eventually admitted to the hospital and tethered to an IV. Rick offered to smuggle into the hospital the heavy, soporific dishes Eric had loved as a child: biscuits with gravy, chicken-fried steak. But the foods he'd once loved revolted him now, and Rick's offer made him feel like a finicky child. "Honey," he told Rick, "it's better if you don't try to feed me." For days Rick sat by the bed while Eric faded in and out of sleep, his meals growing cold. Nurses swept through the room and changed the IV bag dripping into Eric's arm, a clear solution that bypassed the tongue.

Despite daily infusions and the few bites of food he forced himself to eat, Eric was dying of starvation. "AIDS-related wasting," Dr. Santos told Rick in the corridor, "remains one of our most difficult battles." The doctor spoke in a solicitous whisper, but Rick heard surrender ring through the ward, drowning out authority and hope. "Do you understand," asked Dr. Santos, "how wasting works?" Rick knew very well how wasting worked: lips papery, cheeks hollow, eyes puzzled, Eric retreated into the stillness and solitude of his body. No wish or prayer or entreaty could restore him. "What more," he asked the doctor, "do I need to know?"

*　　*　　*

The Westgate Safeway, glaring and imperious, loomed above dozens of smaller shops. Rick pulled in to the lot. On the drive here, he'd had to remind himself that a year had passed since Eric's death. Except for teaching two graduate seminars at a local art school, Rick spent most of that year working on paintings of slender, disconnected bones glowing against a black background. Now that the paintings were being shown in New York, Rick had accepted Jerry's invitation as part of a plan to end his isolation and revive his flagging social life. More than once after leaving the Pillings' house, Rick considered finding the freeway and simply driving back home, five dollars richer, but anything sounded better than returning to an empty studio. Besides, he liked the other guests, and he was curious to see how Jerry fared in his double life. Rick had never met anyone like Meg and Jerry, which accounted for the evening's strain, and also its sense of adventure. *It's only one night,* he told himself, parking the car.

The second he stepped though the supermarket's automatic doors, Rick heard a tune he recognized but couldn't identify, its perky, repetitive rhythms urging him down the aisles. Wandering past shelves stocked with eye-catching cans and packages, Rick became one big, indiscriminate craving. Everything looked appetizing. In the pet food section, basted dog bones seemed like the perfect complement to a sharp Stilton or a salmon pâté. In Household Cleaning Products, pastel kitchen sponges looked as edible as petits-fours. The linoleum throughout the store was creamy white and speckled like spumoni. "Your eyes are bigger than your stomach," he remembered his mother saying when he'd heaped his plate with more than he could eat. Once, he'd learned about the world by putting its pretty objects in his mouth—the dusty taste of a wooden block, a bitter waxy bite of Crayola—and tonight he'd reclaimed, without even trying, this long-lost, infant wisdom.

When he rounded the corner, he caught a glimpse of Jan, in her pinstriped suit, striding toward Gourmet Foods. With his head turned, Rick almost ran into a man who was handing out samples of Inferno Chili. Standing behind a folding table, he wore a white apron and stirred a pot that was heated from beneath by Sterno. Peering inside the pot, Rick saw kidney beans, chunks of tomato, and bits of ruddy onion. The concoction bubbled like lava, small eruptions burping from its surface. "Try some?" asked the man. He held out a plastic spoon, a dollop of chili steaming at its tip, the smell robust and peppery.

Before Rick even began to chew, chili lit the wick of his tongue, his taste buds scorched by exhilarating flame. His eyes watered, his nose ran. Perspiration beaded on his skin. He wrenched the spoon out of his mouth and grabbed a can of the stuff, as if reading the ingredients might explain the unearthly surge of heat. "A taste of hell in every bite!" exclaimed the devil on the label, grinning maliciously. Rick opened his mouth, half expecting to exhale fire and torch the store. The man in the apron handed him a tiny paper cup filled with Gatorade. "Only thing that cuts the burn," he said. "That cayenne's got a kick." When he smiled, wrinkles radiated from his brown eyes. His black mustache was waxed at the ends, his jaw shaped like a horseshoe. Rick wanted to thank him, but his throat had closed, leaving him speechless. "Here's one for the road," said the man, offering Rick another shot. At first, Rick wasn't sure if his gallant, folksy manners were real, or his languorous twang authentic. He studied the man through tearing eyes. His nametag read "Earl." Dazed in the aftermath of chili, cool air wafting from the dairy case, Rick couldn't stop staring.

Ordinarily, Rick wasn't attracted to dark-haired men, or to men with mustaches, especially waxed. Any guy who reminded him of potbellied stoves and tooled-leather belts had always struck him as so remote from his own tastes and sympathies as to be practically extraterrestrial. In the past year, though, every man had seemed alien to Rick because he didn't look or smell like Eric. He'd dated two men since Eric's death, but neither involvement lasted long. In the middle of an intimate dinner, he found himself staring across the table at masticating teeth, tufts of hair on the knuckles of a hand, and though he was glad his companions were mammals, these features were vividly physical without being the least erotic. The one time he did have sex, it was to prove to himself that he could excite someone besides Eric. While flailing naked, he'd inventory the way he and his new partner made love: *Now he's plunging his tongue into my mouth, now I'm licking the inside of his thigh.* He might as well have brought a clipboard to bed. After sex was over, Rick knew he'd been a lousy lover, mired in the past, hopelessly distracted, as spontaneous as a metronome. And now, at the Westgate Safeway of all places, while Muzak tinkled in the glaring air, Rick's desire awoke from hibernation. Earl returned Rick's gaze—there was no mistaking—with the same flirtatious curiosity. "What brings you to the Safeway?" asked Earl as he slowly stirred the Inferno.

Coated with dust, its brown enamel faded by the sun, Earl's ancient station wagon looked like a boulder that had rolled into the parking lot. Rick carried the folding table and cooking equipment while Earl gripped a cardboard box filled with cans of Inferno. Now that Earl had taken off his apron, Rick could better see the outline of his body and the motion of his ropy limbs. Earl propped the boxes on the roof of the car and fished in his jeans pocket for keys. The Golden State Freeway roared in the distance. "By the way," said Earl, "you can keep your five bucks; there's no finer way to promote a product than feeding it directly to the people."

"It isn't my money," Rick reminded him. "And besides, Inferno will be the bargain of the party." They lifted the tailgate, loaded the car. As they slid inside and slammed their doors, the station wagon creaked on its springs. "Just throw that crap in the back," said Earl. "I wasn't expecting company." Rick reached down and chucked cans of Sterno, a box of plastic spoons, and a stack of paper cups into the backseat. Crumpled McDonald's bags and a few empty soft-drink bottles littered the floor. Rick told Earl that the station wagon reminded him of his studio when he was too steeped in work to think about cleaning, to give order to anything but art; the disarray was industrious. "I guess I can see that," said Earl, nodding at the compliment and idling the engine. "It's in me to give a thing my all. Before selling Inferno, I did a stint at a pitiful little radio station in Buford. My spot was called *The Classical Half-Hour,* but it was more like a fancy fifteen minutes. I'll tell you, though, this gig's as solitary as being a DJ. During long hauls, I've been known to interrogate myself just to have a conversation." Earl laughed and shook his head. "The things you'll confess, alone on the road." He twisted a knob on the dashboard and a tape deck sputtered to life. "Johann Sebastian Bach," said Earl, upping the volume. "Best antidote I know to a day of Muzak." He threw the station wagon into reverse.

"Do you know your way around Westgate?" asked Rick.

"All I know these days are supermarkets. Everyplace in between is just gas stations and motels. Don't you know where we're headed?"

The directions were locked in Rick's car back at the lot and, after convincing Earl to keep him company, he wasn't about to suggest they turn around. Rick peered through the bird droppings and insect remains that splattered the windshield, doing his best to guess the way back to Meg and Jerry's. He couldn't help but interpret the windshield as a good omen: Earl had traveled numberless gritty miles to meet him, and even if they only spent one night together, the unlikelihood of their having met, combined with the tape deck's welling arpeggios, made their impromptu date seem predestined. "It's funny," said Earl, "to have a passenger." As Rick leaned toward the dash and squinted at street signs, he told Earl about his conversation with Jerry on the plane. All the while, he could sense Earl staring. Lack of subtlety was one of Earl's most appealing traits, and Rick had to use every ounce of restraint and concentration to keep his mind on the road. But when Earl rested his hand on Rick's thigh, Rick dove headfirst into the driver's seat, yanked Earl's shirt from his jeans, and licked his stomach, the flesh warm, taut, and salty. Earl gasped and arched his back, allowing Rick to lift his shirt higher. Rick pulled his head back far enough to see Earl's stomach in the emerald light of the dashboard. Wind from the open windows ruffled Rick's hair and blew into his shirt; the velocity of the car, the rumble of the engine, the bumps in the road felt metabolic. "That," he said, peering up from Earl's lap, "is one beautiful bellybutton." Rick couldn't help but notice that the things he said and did that night were unlike him, or at least unlike the recluse he'd become, and his audacity, like a file baked in a cake, freed him from the cell of himself. He circled and probed Earl's navel with his tongue.

"Yikes," heaved Earl. "You *are* an artist!" He steered the car to the side of the road with one hand and gripped a hank of Rick's hair with the other, pressing him against his stomach. The station wagon grazed the curb and lurched to a stop, its cargo rolling and clattering in the back.

Earl's mouth was wet and generous, his hard jaw covered with stubble. When he moaned, his bony chest rattled with pleasure, an erection tenting his jeans. The more they kissed, the more Rick realized how alone he'd been, and the more alone he realized he'd been, the greedier his kisses became. The restless pressure of Earl's hands had the power to cause and alleviate need. Finally, the two of them pulled apart long enough to catch their breath and make a plan: an appearance at the potluck, back to the Safeway for condoms and Rick's car, then on to Earl's motel.

After ringing the doorbell, the two of them waited on the front stoop, cooking equipment in tow. As Rick reached out to squeeze Earl's shoulder, he remembered reaching beneath Eric's sweatshirt and rubbing the supple muscles of his back. The memory, blunt and unbidden, lingered in his hands.

When no one answered the door, they sneaked inside the house as quietly as thieves. In the living room, Earl's eyes widened. "Beats the rooms at Best Western." The guests had gathered in the dining room, where sliding glass doors opened onto the backyard and the luminous pool. Even from a distance, Rick could hear the strain of people trying to keep the ball of small talk aloft. A surprised hush greeted Rick as he walked into the room with a stranger. Everyone eyed them quizzically. Rick apologized for being late and introduced Earl all around, counting on the possibility that the Pillings were too bent on being "outlandish," and too constrained by good manners, to object to an uninvited guest. "I sure appreciate the invitation," Earl said to Meg. There had been no invitation, of course, but Earl's gratitude disarmed Mrs. Pilling. "We're glad to have you," she said uncertainly.

Meg had set the table in anticipation of a buffet. The white tablecloth matched the napkins fanned atop it. Empty china bowls and plates shone beneath the chandelier. Rick had to admit that Earl, a stewpot dangling from his arm, made a scruffy addition to the pristine room and the well-dressed guests. Earl was a wild card, a complete stranger who was capable, Rick realized with both alarm and excitement, of almost anything. As a result of their feverish making out, Earl's hair was mussed, his mustache frayed. Rick didn't dare imagine what *he* looked like, though he suspected a hickey was imprinted on his neck. Propped against Rick's chest was a cardboard box. He set it on the table and explained that, for a mere five dollars, Earl was going to treat them to an up-and-coming American meal.

"Up-and-coming, indeed," repeated Oscar, who could skew any phrase toward innuendo.

Rick shot Oscar a warning glance.

Earl cleared his throat, straightened up, and mustered all the salesmanship he had left. "This is just about the most savory pot of chili you'll ever taste," he said in his polished, disc-jockey modulations. "Inferno's aiming for a three-year growth plan with a product-recognition goal along the lines of, say, your Dinty Moore or Del Monte." He lit a fire beneath the pot and began stacking cans of Inferno into a pyramid, display-style. "We've got quite a few backers in South Dallas, the kind of ranchers who're all wallet and no cows."

Mitchell smiled for the first time that night and Rick was sure he found Earl attractive. Jerry saw Mitchell smiling at Earl, and his body tensed. It occurred to Rick that Jerry might harbor a secret crush; didn't Mitchell possess the collegiate look, glasses and all, that had made the airborne Jerry rhapsodic? Noticing the devil on the cans, Meg folded her arms and turned to share a look of consternation with her husband. When Meg saw Jerry staring at his dentist, the same hunch that occurred to Rick seemed to cross her mind. Her arms slipped loose and fell to her sides.

This was the aspect of parties that Rick found most wondrous and suffocating: one suddenly became entangled in the invisible lines of lust or envy or resentment that stretched between the guests. Suddenly, Rick was walloped by an idea: a diagram of the party would be his next painting! He saw, against a backdrop of muddy color, filaments of glowing emotion.

Once Earl had completed his pitch, the others took turns presenting their purchases. Jan dredged from a Safeway bag, one by one, a can of baby corncobs, a tin of Norwegian sardines, and a glass jar crammed with tiny white cocktail onions that, even beneath the flattering light of the chandelier, looked haplessly subterranean. She placed the offerings on the table. Everyone eyed the foreign labels. "It's gor-may," she enunciated. "I once had a girlfriend who lived for pickled foods." Meg blushed, as if "pickled foods" were a euphemism. Jerry began to struggle with the jar of onions, huffing and gritting his teeth until Jan grabbed it from his hand and twisted off the lid with a flick of her wrist. "You loosened it for me," she told him, and Rick imagined that she'd had to say that, or something equally reassuring, to many men in order to downplay her prowess and spare them embarrassment. She dumped the onions into a bowl.

Mitchell contributed three boxes of Lunchables, a packaged assortment of lunch meats, crackers, and processed cheese spreads that could be served in various combinations. He ripped open the boxes and, hunched in an occupational posture, prepared a plate of meticulous hors d'oeuvres.

Oscar proffered a one-pound box of marzipan from Heidi's Kandy Kitchen, a concession he'd found tucked away in a strip mall. Everyone oohed at the replicas of ripe fruit, the box exuding a sweet almond odor. Meg said, "They're precious," and gingerly nibbled a miniature orange. What happened next was something that Rick, who considered himself visually sophisticated, if not downright jaded, had never conceived of, let alone seen. Meg let loose a warble of horror and her right eyelid began to widen and contract, the eyeball adrift in its socket. Her otherwise mild and maternal presence gave way to a kind of lascivious rapture, and if Meg hadn't been mortified into silence, Rick would have expected her to purr with delight, lick her own shoulder, or nip at the air. The instant Jerry became aware of what was happening, he pulled out a chair, into which Meg plummeted. With one hand she applied pressure to her tremulous brow, and with the other held her eyelid closed by the lashes. While she was trying without success to control her eye, her jaw went lax and revealed a mash of marzipan. When Meg realized she was flashing food at her stunned guests, she shut her mouth with such force, her teeth snapped together like the clasp of a purse.

"Oh, my God!" yelped Mitchell. "I read about it in dental school but I've never seen it happen firsthand!"

"What is it?" barked Jan. She stood erect and ready, as though prepared to pin Mrs. Pilling to the floor if the spasms worsened.

Meg waved her hand as if to say, *Don't look at me, please.*
Everyone crowded closer.

The body is such a mystery, thought Rick; *you forget that your
eyes are apertures, that your skin is a huge and vulnerable organ,
that your muscles have a will of their own.*

Mitchell bent over Meg. "Is it Marcus Gunn reflex?" he
asked.

Meg nodded.

"You've heard of it?" marveled Jerry. "I'm very impressed."
He dashed through the swinging door and retrieved a glass of
water from the kitchen. While Meg took a couple of grateful
gulps, Jerry rested his hands on her shoulders, his wedding band
catching the light. "Hasn't happened in years, has it, darling?"

Meg poked and kneaded her own cheek as if putting the
finishing touches on a clay bust. "I think it's stopped," she
said. The guests gazed at Mrs. Pilling and waited to see if the
twitching returned. A warm breeze blew through the screen
doors. A swing set clanked in the backyard. Crickets throbbed
on the lawns of Westgate. At last, Mitchell pronounced the
episode over and there came a collective murmur of relief.

"Marcus Gunn reflex is rare," explained Mitchell. "It's
caused when the chewing muscles and salivary glands are connected to the muscles that control the eyes. Anything can set it
off: certain kinds of food, emotional stress, even novocaine in-
jected into the wrong spot."

"It's painless," said Meg, "but unpredictable and terribly
embarrassing."

"And congenital," added Jerry. "Her mother first noticed it
when she was nursing Meg in the hospital. 'It made my baby
look like a little sucking glutton,' she used to tell me. 'So bliss-
ful at the teat.'"

Meg twisted around and glared at Jerry. "Thank you," she said. She took a deep breath and hoisted herself out of the chair. "Will you all excuse me." Meg fled into the kitchen. Jerry hurried after her. No sooner had the swinging door stilled than there arose the angry clank of pots, a furious blast of tap water. Rick realized with a wince that the Pillings weren't familiar with the acoustics of their new kitchen—all that decoy noise did little to mask their voices. "I'm embarrassed enough as it is, Jerry, without you regaling your friends with stories about my breast-feeding. They don't have to know everything about me."

"What do you mean, 'embarrassed enough as it is'?"

"I can't look at those people without thinking about what they do with each other in bed."

Oscar sighed a facetious sigh. "One look at me and people think of sex."

"They don't do anything with each other," said Jerry. "They didn't even know each other until tonight."

Jan peeled the lid from the tin of sardines. A regiment of fish stared back, darkly iridescent. "What are these marinated in anyway?" she asked. "Motor oil?"

Earl surveyed the buffet. "This," he said, "is one cocka-mamie potluck." He hummed under his breath and dished chili into the bowls.

"'Luck' is the operative word in 'potluck,'" mused Oscar. "On the groaning board before you, what looks like mere food is actually the manifestation of chance." He waved a hand over the table. "Things come together in ways you'd never expect."

"And fall apart in ways you'd never expect," added Mitchell.

"Then don't think about what they do in bed, Meg."

"I can't be around them and *not* think about it. That's the problem with homosexuals."

"But this party was your idea as much as mine."

"No, Jerry. It was *your* idea. I agreed to this party because, after consulting with the elders, I was ready to do whatever it took to live up to our vows, to keep you happy and faithful. But you know what I found out tonight, Jerry? I found out I'm old-fashioned. And I'm tired of being polite. Men lying with men, women with women: it's a sin, period. And you condone it." Silverware clanked like scrap metal. "I saw you looking at that Mitchell."

Mitchell took a bite of chili and his eyes began to water. "Even if I were attracted to Jerry," he said, "I'd never date a patient. Especially not a heterosexual. It's hard enough to find someone compatible; why would I want to make the odds impossible by going after a straight man? Besides, abscesses and gum recession don't exactly fan the flames of lust." He sniffed, removed a handkerchief from his back pocket, and blew his nose. "This is delicious," he said to Earl.

"Jerry was cruising the pants off you," said Oscar. "The man could use a few lessons in the art of the clandestine glance. Especially if he plans to stay married." He surveyed the table. "Meg is a lovely woman when she's not besieged by queers."

"Besieged?" said Rick. "I seem to recall being invited."

"In Texas," said Earl, "the married ones go to another town when they want to fool around. They'll do everything with another man but kiss him on the lips, and they think that makes them . . ."

"Pure as the driven snow," said Oscar. "It's amazing, all the intimate things you can do with another human being and still remain a virgin."

"Don't tell me you weren't ogling him," said Meg. "I have eyes."

"That's an understatement," said Oscar.

Jan fished a baby corncob from a bowl. "Hold on, you guys. I don't blame her for being upset. It's another case of the wife getting the short end of the stick. I'm awfully fond of Jerry, but at the office, he's one of the boys when he's with gay men and one of the men when he's with straight women." She poked the cob—a pale, extraneous finger—into the air for emphasis. "Jerry wants it both ways, which would be harmless, I guess, unless you were married to him and had a horde of kids to take care of. None of us would want to be in Meg's position."

"Of course not," said Rick. "But the way Jerry explained it . . ."

Meg hissed, "You twist things around till they suit you."

"I'm trying to do what's best for—"

"—me and the kids? Spare me the piety, Jerry."

"For all of us, I was going to say. So I think a man is handsome; what's that have to do with how I feel about you?"

"Nothing," said Meg. "And it hurts."

"I know what Jerry's going through," said Mitchell. "My ex-wife is still furious because I told her I was gay. And because I didn't tell her sooner."

"In other words," said Oscar, "she's mad at you for failing at the marriage *and* for trying to make it work."

A glass broke in the kitchen. "Look what you made me do," shrilled Meg.

Mitchell gazed into his plate. "Do you think we should leave?"

"Not me," said Rick. "I don't care if they start throwing knives. I've waited all night to eat and I'm not going anywhere until I'm full." He loaded his bowl, took Earl by the hand, and walked outside. At the pool's edge, Rick and Earl yanked off their shoes and socks. They dangled their legs in the tepid water and shared the bowl of finger food. "Sure would be nice to stay in one place for a while," Earl lamented. "Tomorrow I've got a gig at a Market Basket in Placerville." Rick might have felt a pang of sadness about Earl's leaving, but the temperate air, the plentiful stars, and the pool as bright and fathomless as daylight fortified him against despair. *Compared to losing Eric,* he thought, *all my future losses are bound to be bearable.* The second he thought this, he knew it wasn't true. "I wish I lived here," said Earl. "This would be a good place to stay put." His words were so plaintive, so burdened with yearning, that Rick laughed when Earl added, "But then I'd probably be in the kitchen scrapping with my wife."

Oscar and Mitchell and Jan walked toward the pool, a talkative trio. Each of them held a china plate filled with incongruous food. Rick recognized in their speech and gestures small flourishes of good will—a stray touch, a teasing retort—that a stranger might mistake for flirtation. When Jan delivered the punch line of a joke—"And the priest says, 'Young lady, when you get to heaven, St. Finger is going to wag his peter at you'"—laughter replaced the silence of the night. Somehow a party had sprouted in the Pillings' backyard like a dandelion through a crack in the sidewalk. Rick leaned against Earl, swinging his legs until waves slapped at the sides of the pool, rafts and life buoys drifting on the choppy turquoise currents.

The sound of churning water drew two of the Pillings' children from their rooms. They materialized from behind the swing set at the far end of the house. The youngest, a barefoot girl in an oversize T-shirt—Rick guessed her to be about ten—sauntered toward the strangers. She plunked herself down by the water and tried to garner, without seeming to, as much attention as possible. When the inflatable shark drifted toward her, she flung out a leg and kicked it in the snout. The shark wheezed and sailed away. "I'm Yvonne," she announced.

"That's not her real name," said the boy from the opposite side of the pool, hands thrust in his pockets. Rick had no trouble imagining him as a grown man who inhabited the periphery of parties, lobbing skeptical remarks into the crowd, eyes animated by the same watchfulness that shone in them tonight.

"I'm the governess," said the girl.

"She's my little sister," corrected the boy. "She likes to act bratty and pretend she's things she's not."

The girl went on, undaunted. "Are you friends of Mr. and Mrs. Pilling?"

The guests paused, considering her question.

"Excuse us" came the voices of Meg and Jerry from inside the dining room. Everyone turned to face them. Jerry stared forlornly into the backyard, as if he were outside the house looking in. "I'm afraid it's late," he said, pointing to his watch. Meg said, "We hate to be party poopers." Their voices, as if strained through the wire mesh of the screen doors, were timid and thin.

Rick and Earl shook water from their feet and, while lacing their shoes, glanced at each other with such overt erotic promise, Oscar clicked his tongue.

Jan and Mitchell hurried their conversation, determined to fit in a few remarks before parting. "I bet your ex-wife will be more forgiving when she finds another husband," said Jan. "If I knew more heterosexual men, I'd set her up on a blind date." Mitchell agreed that things would be easier once she was coupled, but behind the gold-rimmed glasses, his eyes conveyed their native doubt.

The little girl and her brother bolted across the concrete, flung open the screen doors, and ran into the dining room. Yvonne nearly collided with her father, embracing his leg, and Rick wondered what it would be like to be grabbed by your brash and affectionate child just when love seemed most far-fetched. The boy gravitated toward his mother but remained aloof. Ever the considerate hostess, Meg flicked on the outdoor light, a magnet drawing moths whose frantic shadows churned against the house.

"Shall we take our leave?" asked Oscar. And the visitors headed inside.

Rick received a postcard from Arizona that depicted a jackelope, the imaginary offspring of an antelope and a jackrabbit. A postcard from Florida showed a freight train's flatcar loaded with an orange the size of a house. Earl sent the most surreal cards he could find, either because he favored them or because he thought they'd appeal to the artist in Rick. They arrived every few weeks, a reminder that the world's oddities were inexhaustible.

Eventually, however, the cards stopped coming, as Rick knew they would. Earl never asked for a reply or included a return address. Besides, Rick was at work on a new painting and, apart from a nagging set of technical and aesthetic preoccupations, he had little to talk about. He'd come to think of his encounter with Earl as a thing completed, an improvised composition that one more brushstroke would ruin.

And then, just as Rick was about to relegate his evening in Westgate to the past, a letter arrived from Meg and Jerry. It was one of those Xeroxed family newsletters sent out at Christmas.

Listed in alphabetical order were the academic and athletic victories of the Pillings' six children. Rick noted with amusement that there was no mention of a girl named Yvonne. Apart from parental hyperbole, the highlights of Meg and Jerry's year were reserved for the last two sentences: "We visited the Big Island of Hawaii in September, where we glimpsed the fury of a live volcano. Upon our return, Jerry assumed a position on the church's high council."

Rick turned the letter over, searching for a salutation scrawled in the margins, or for some note that would say what had become of Jerry and whether his equivocations persisted. But the margins were empty and even the signatures were photocopied. Rick slid the Pillings' letter into the rolltop desk he'd inherited from Eric, and swiveled around to face his latest painting. The cavernous studio contained a commotion of paintbrushes, dropcloths, and coffee cans encrusted with acrylics. Beyond the windows, sunlight burned through passing clouds, then slid over streets and billboards and buildings. The fluid, moody light animated his painting. Its imagery was based on his recollection of Saturday morning cartoons in which trails of enticing odor wafted from hot pies or freshly baked bread; then as now, he loved how they rippled through a room to caress a face, burrow into nostrils, and beckon the hungry with curling fingers. Follow. Taste. Be sated. Rick leaned forward. Thanks to hours spent feathering wet paint with a small brush, tendrils of scent reached across the canvas. One moment they seemed to float closer. The next they seemed to recede.

a man in the making

Mark curled on the living room couch in his pajamas and re-minded himself to cough. He drew the old wedding quilt, with its pattern of pale, fraying circles, up to his chin. The family station wagon idled in the driveway, vibrations from its engine causing his mother's knickknacks—silver spoons from Niagara Falls, demure porcelain courtiers—to clatter in the mahogany cabinet. Mrs. Kern hovered above him and asked again if he had a fever. "Not yet," he said. Across the room hung a portrait of Christ, a nimbus of light surrounding his head. "I wish I could go," Mark told his mother, both amazed and ashamed at his easy lie. "Keep warm," said Mrs. Kern, "and climb into bed if you get really bad." She made a move to reach down and lay a hand on her son's forehead or tuck him securely beneath the quilt, but her thin arms returned to her sides. She restrained herself from such gestures now that he was thirteen, mostly on the advice of her husband, who believed that pampering softened a boy, especially a mother's touch.

Outside, Mr. Kern honked the horn in two short bursts and Peter, Mark's older brother, shouted for his mom to hurry. "The patient in spirit," mumbled Mrs. Kern, "are finer than the proud in spirit." When she turned in the doorway to wave good-bye, the gold letters of her hymnal glinted in the morning light.

The chiming knickknacks quieted. Without lifting his head from the pillow, Mark knew his parents and brother were gone. He coughed an unconvincing cough, trying not to meet Christ's eyes. It's just a painting, he said to himself. Though he'd waited all week for privacy, Mark had forgotten that, once he was alone, the world would be emptied of everything but his longing, which swept now through the small stucco house and heated his skin like fever.

He threw off the quilt and ran to the bedroom he shared with Peter. The doll sat at the bottom of the cedar trunk in which Peter, who'd recently turned fifteen, kept the belongings he'd outgrown and yet was too fond of to give to his younger brother or donate to the church: model airplanes, firecrackers from Mexico, dog-eared baseball cards. Digging through the trunk, dizzy with anticipation, Mark tried to remember the exact order of its contents, worried that a misplaced box might arouse his brother's suspicion. He could picture, with alarming clarity, every mistake he might make during his ritual: leaving the lid of the trunk ajar or putting the doll's pants on backwards. Even the most far-fetched possibilities—speaking the doll's name in his sleep, say—crossed his mind and taunted him. Every night he closed his eyes and, with a concentration that could have passed for prayer, wished he didn't need the doll.

There existed in his shame one consolation: the Four Square Gospel service, with its frantic goings-on, had shown Mark that others also lost control. When the spirit touched his parents and his brother, their eyes rolled back and their bodies shuddered, tongues letting loose a torrent of words. Mrs. Kern was touched especially often. Preacher Addington, a jowly, kinetic man who wore the same white suit and shiny tie every Sunday, would rush up to his swaying mother and press his palms against her jaws. "Let the Spirit enter!" he'd bark. She'd smile faintly and tip back on her heels, and two of Addington's handlers would lower her onto the floor. As soon as Mrs. Kern was horizontal, Preacher Addington shot across the room, the handlers racing after him to catch another congregant. Mark would brace himself against the back of a pew as he watched his mother shout gibberish and writhe in the aisle. He envied her swift oblivion, yet fought the urge to lift her up, to free her from the grip of her seizure.

Occasionally, old Mr. Pierce presumed to translate his mother's heavenly blather into plain English. He'd totter over from his seat in the first row, cocking his head so he might better hear Mrs. Kern through his good ear. Furrowing his brow, Pierce made all the thoughtful faces of an elder privy to important news. "Sustain your faith," he was likely to say in his tremulous voice, or "Forgive the people who have burdened your heart with sadness or anger." Mark had grown increasingly suspicious of Mr. Pierce's skill as a translator—or else the Lord was repeating Himself week after week. Mark had considered mentioning this to his mother, but Mrs. Kern neither remembered nor seemed the least interested in what she'd said, or what the Spirit said through her. "Being struck by his touch," she once told him, "is reward enough."

One Sunday last spring, Mark had felt the Spirit enter him. Preacher Addington shouted, "Lift up your eyes, lift up your hearts, lift up your hands!" with such conviction, Mark found himself rising to his feet and closing his eyes. In the darkness he lost his sense of direction, could feel the bass notes of Addington's words shake the church loose from its foundations and lift it slowly into the air. The thought of it made him smile like his mother, the smile of the righteous. *It's happening,* he said to himself, and he hoped his mother, standing beside him, would turn his way and notice. While Opal Addington pounded out "He's the Rock of My Salvation" on an upright piano, the murmurs and yelps of the congregation swelled like a wave and broke over his body, entering every orifice and pore, filling him with an exaltation too great to bear. Mark was a vessel for the language of the Lord. How could he not have known this before, the purpose of his lungs, the reason for his voice? His lips parted, his throat opened. But what came forth was halting nonsense, all baby talk and fakery. Light flickered on the underside of his eyelids and he was afraid that, unless he kept them closed, they might fly open and reveal the familiar, earthbound room and his mother's disappointed face. He continued to let the words trickle out, but his voice had faded to an uninspired whisper. When at last he gave up and opened his eyes, he saw his mother, and the rest of the Four Square congregation, standing with their arms held high and swaying like a field of wheat.

The smell of cedar rose from the depths of the trunk. Kneeling on the floor, blood banging in his temples, Mark fished out the box and removed its lid. Only when his eyes met the doll's did he allow himself to speak the name: Guy Joe. He knew that "G.I." stood for "government issue," but he liked the two letters better as a word. He thought of Guy Joe as a "doll," which sounded more exciting—blunt and forbidden—than "Action Soldier," as written on the side of the box. Mark replaced the other toys and quietly closed the trunk.

He clutched Guy Joe and hurried down the hall. Once inside his parents' bedroom, Mark pulled open the top drawer of the dresser. His mother had balled his father's socks and arranged them in neat rows. Mark deliberated for a moment, especially drawn to the blacks and browns that hadn't faded despite his mother's almost daily trips to the washing machine in the basement. By removing a pair, he ruined his mother's handiwork, like a finger gouging a frosted cake. Even this small and secret act confirmed the large and frightening fact that his longing led to the end of order.

Now that he had the doll and the socks, Mark headed toward the kitchen and the only messy drawer in the house, a bird's nest of odds and ends. In it, he found the bottle of Elmer's Glue and a stubby white candle, its wick black from last time. There were a few matchbooks to choose from—the Pepper Pot, Kelly's Steak House—souvenirs from his parents' rare nights out on the town.

Mark set the doll on the kitchen table and lined up beside it the glue, socks, candle, and matches. Though his mother had washed the dishes that morning, the kitchen still smelled of frying bacon. Mark opened the window above the sink; the scent of breakfast made him feel less private, reminded him that others lived in this house. Away at Sunday prayer meeting, his family couldn't possibly know what he was doing, yet their disapproval seemed to linger along with the odor of food. Through the open window, beyond the Kerns' front yard, hundreds of homes exactly like Mark's sprawled beneath the San Gabriel Mountains.

He pulled up a chair and undid the snaps of Joe's camouflage fatigues, worried that the men at Hasbro hadn't planned for the pants to come off so often. *There are no boys,* he could almost hear them say, *who would want to undress a soldier.* What Mark became as he stripped Joe's clothes was different from other boys.

Joe was easy to pose in the stances of battle: throwing a hand grenade, aiming a bayonet, driving a jeep. "America's moveable fighting man," it said in the booklet. "Made of durable plastic, G.I. Joe has been specially designed so that he can assume positions that a real life Marine can. Hips swivel all around! Wrists move forward and back! Ankles bend!" The advantage of an agile man: you can make him do whatever you want.

The green plastic fatigue cap and the little dog tag came off without a hitch. Mark set them atop the camouflage fatigues, which he'd neatly folded like his own clothes when he went to Dr. Berry's for a check-up. Joe's boots were another matter. They didn't unlace, and had to be grasped at the heel and yanked off. But the more of Guy Joe's body he exposed, the less control Mark had of his hands; they grew rubbery and weak with excitement. Joe's foot came off with a sickening pop. Mark grabbed a fork from the silverware drawer and jimmied the stubborn appendage from the boot, snapping it back onto Guy Joe's ankle.

Whenever something went wrong during his ritual—what lengths he went to for satisfaction!—Mark lamented the absence of arousing images in the house. Sometimes his father flipped past wrestlers on TV, and Mark would fix the men in his mind, muscled and grunting and tangled in a headlock. In the back pages of his mother's *Good Housekeeping* magazine, he once found an advertisement for a resort in Mexico that showed a couple lounging on a beach, the husband's body a tiny enticement. Then there were the illustrations of Jesus in almost every book the Kerns owned, his skin smooth and pale, his willowy body spilling from the shroud as he ascended to heaven. As sinful as it was for Mark to admit that he was aware of Christ's body, it was almost worse to admit that he didn't find the Lord all that handsome.

Mark liked robust and hairy men. Take Mr. Simmons, the political science teacher, who lived across the street. Ordinarily, Simmons wore baggy suits, sucked a pipe, and gave long, impromptu lectures on current events to anyone within earshot. "Do you follow me?" he'd always ask, a puff of tobacco hanging in the air. On warm Saturdays, however, Mr. Simmons underwent a transformation more startling than Clark Kent's. That was when Mr. Simmons mowed his front lawn and, soaked with perspiration, peeled off his shirt. Pressed against a window across the street, Mark stared at the body suits had hidden—light under a bushel. Luxurious fur matted Mr. Simmons's chest and covered his sinewy forearms. As he pushed a ratcheting hand mower, his ruddy skin glistened in the sunlight, clouds of grass spraying from the blades.

Mark lit a match and touched it to the wick. Tilting the small glass candleholder, he dripped hot wax onto the flat patch of Guy Joe's crotch. Working quickly so the wax would remain pliable, Mark molded an erect penis, tall or thick or lopsided depending on his whims and the steadiness of his hand.

As the penis hardened, he shaped and smoothed it like a sand-castle. He made testicles, too, blowing to cool them off before they ran in rivulets down Guy Joe's thighs.

With a firm squeeze, a moist white bead bubbled to the tip of the glue bottle. Mark dabbed it at strategic points over Joe's body. He plucked brown fuzz from his father's socks and patted it into the doll's armpits. Next he fashioned a hairy chest. This narrowed into a trail of hair that descended toward the navel, growing plush again above the genitalia. Since he had time to spare (the glue would stay tacky for about fifteen minutes before it dried) he gave Guy Joe a hasty beard.

Mark stood the doll on the table, its arms outstretched. As he petted the swaths of hair with one hand, he plunged the other down his pajamas. With every stroke, every shift in pressure and tempo, all his strength flooded his groin, the rest of him quaking.

And just as Mark teetered on the verge of orgasm, he heard a faint chiming from the next room: the sound of his mother's knickknacks rattling in the cabinet. The family station wagon had pulled into the driveway. Slammed back to his senses, he stood up so fast the room swooned in circles. He grabbed the lit candle but, burned by hot wax, he dropped it again. His wince sent the matchbook skidding off the kitchen table and across the floor. Scooping all the props into his arms, he lurched into the living room, penis still erect, and saw his mother's silhouette rippling across a curtain and moving toward the porch.

He had no idea why they'd returned or what room she might go to, but the basement seemed like her least likely destination. There, he could stay out of sight long enough to hide Guy Joe. Of course, his mother would want to know what on earth he was doing in the basement, barefoot no less, and coming down with a cold. He figured he'd think of a good excuse; didn't the hairy man in his arms prove he'd become an expert at invention?

Mark shouldered open the basement door, panting hard. Behind him, at the other end of the living room, he heard the key turn in the lock. The steep staircase with its runner of old carpet descended into darkness. Dank, subterranean air wafted toward him and carried with it the faint odor of laundry detergent. There wasn't time to grope for the light switch, and so he took a step on faith.

Plunging down the stairs headfirst, his arms grasped at empty air, striking the wall and the banister. Every step was a blow to his back, breath after breath pummeled from his lungs. Even then he didn't let go of the doll. The last thing he felt was its fur against his fingers, the only thing soft in the gauntlet of his fall.

A blast of light. The muted edges of another dimension. Far below him, at the bottom of a cataract, his mother calls him back to the world. If his tongue could move he'd tell her not to worry. How dreamy and remote he feels. He holds a miniature man in his hand, newly minted, as naked as Adam. He wants to tell her, *Look what I made.*

Soon his father appears beside his mother. His brother peeks above their shoulders, standing on his toes. Mouths are moving, eyes wild. The hiss of blood coursing through his ears grows higher and finer and fades away. Then his parents have swooped upon him. "Can you hear me?" shouts his mother, who takes him by the feet. "Can you move?" shouts his father, who takes him by the head. The stairwell's bare bulb glares upon them, their faces brimming with confusion and fear.

Back in a body, Mark starts to cry.

Mr. and Mrs. Kern lumbered up the stairs with Mark slung between them, aching and alert. Staring up at the sunlit ceiling, he was horrified to realize that he still held Guy Joe. Peter lunged forward and snatched the doll. Mark had been more than willing to surrender Guy Joe—surely his parents had noticed the doll, and the less they saw of it, the better—but as he loosened his fingers, letting go, tufts of brown hair clung to his palm. He felt the sticky, bristling growth, but didn't dare raise his hand to look. He made a fist and kept the hair hidden.

Mark's parents settled him on the couch, covered him with the quilt, and propped his head on the pillow. As soon as they went to phone Dr. Berry, Mark peeked at his palm. He made a move to pluck off the hair with his other hand and discovered the fingers were unbendable, numb. Resigned for the moment, he buried his arm beneath the quilt and tried to figure out what to do. What if Dr. Berry insisted on taking his pulse and, forced to comply, Mark unfurled a hairy hand? He could see Dr. Berry's calm blue eyes turn disdainful, knowing the cause of this condition without having to perform any tests or consult a medical text.

While his parents were busy trying to convince Dr. Berry's switchboard that the accident warranted a house call, Mark wedged his hand between the sofa cushions and scraped his palm as hard as he could. Jesus Christ glared from the wall, and Mark couldn't help but interpret this predicament as a holy comeuppance. With every exertion, his shoulder throbbed and he thought he might start to cry again, but he stayed as deter-mined as an injured boy could be; someday his mother would lift the cushion, vacuuming the crusty brown fuzz without a second thought.

In fact, the evidence of Mark's ritual vanished that very night. Mrs. Kern came upon a pair of balled socks in a corner of the basement and thought she'd dropped them while doing the laundry. His father found the book of matches and tossed it back in the kitchen drawer. To spare Mark embarrassment, Peter had either hidden the doll or thrown it away, and there arose between the brothers a tacit understanding that Peter wouldn't say what became of the doll and Mark would never ask.

Dr. Berry diagnosed Mark's injuries as "extensive but mi-nor" and advised plenty of rest. Confined to the house, he couldn't escape his mother's concern. "How's your back?" she'd ask. He'd turn around and hoist his shirt, afraid the sight of his numerous bruises would lead to questions he didn't want to answer. Mrs. Kern would reach toward her son, then hesitate. "The Lord is going to heal you," she'd say.

"How do you know?" Mark asked one day.

Mrs. Kern searched his eyes. "Aren't there things you just know?"

Mark nodded.

"It's like the hymn says when we pass the collection plate, 'We give thee but thine own / A trust, O Lord, from thee . . .'" Mark shrank at the thought of the velvet-lined bowl, the whis-per of paper money; forgetting their tithe was what had brought his family back to the house that day. "If we heed Je-sus like a husband or a father, if we give ourselves over body and soul, we'll be filled to the brim with his joy."

Mark blushed, tucked his shirt back into his pants.

Except for Mrs. Kern's inquiries about his bruises, a spell of silence descended on the house. Every day was momentous because it carried him further away from humiliation. That no one in his family mentioned the circumstances surrounding his fall led Mark to believe that it might not have been the dead giveaway he at first supposed; maybe, by some miracle, they hadn't guessed what he'd been up to. Or else his family's silence was meant to protect him from their pity and disgust. In either case, the magnitude of the accident didn't match their lack of reaction, and eventually, between his family's silence and his will to forget, he began to wonder if Dr. Berry really had made a house call and probed his back—"Any tenderness?"—with hands that Mark worried he liked too much. Had he masturbated with the doll? Didn't he have a fever that day? How could he trust what little he recalled?

Still, Mark found himself watching his family, braced for changes in the way they behaved toward him. On a stifling night toward the end of June, he sat cross-legged on the floor of the dimly lit living room, guzzling a soda while Peter and his parents watched *The Oral Roberts Hour* on television. As they listened to a hymn, Mr. Kern's usually stern expression relaxed into reverence. Mrs. Kern pressed a hand upon her Bible, as though she were swearing an oath in court. Peter muttered "Amen" and "Yes," and Mark understood, with a pang of envy, that these praises came as readily as breath. Mark noticed that Peter had inherited his parents' sharp features, and he reached up to feel his own face, trying to read the Braille of kinship.

It was only a few years ago that Mark had recited Scripture by heart, patiently waiting to know the full extent of the Lord's love. Those recitations allied him with Peter and made his parents sigh with pride. But a dozen nagging details—the Lord's dubious mouthpiece in the form of Mr. Pierce, Preacher Adding-ton's pleasure when scolding the unfaithful, and most of all his own thrill at the bodies of men—had worn down his convic-tion like grains of sand eroding a rock. The rock of salvation.

Oral Roberts's impassioned voice—"Blessed are ye when men shall revile you!"—rose above the chords of a rumbling pipe organ. Mark willed the sermon to stir him, sensed a flicker of his old conviction. In this dark room, on this hot night, see-ing his family bathed in blue light, how could he refuse their blessed assurance?

Mark went to bed contented, but only hours later, he awoke from a dream in which Guy Joe had been out in the open all along, as common as a telephone or lamp, and no one in his family seemed to mind. Sleepless in the June heat, he lay there lamenting their separation, unable to recall Joe's face or his flexible pink physique. This forgetfulness pained him, made him lonely. The only antidote was to close his eyes and imag-ine Mr. Simmons, whose tireless lawn mowing had been the highlight of Mark's summer. In fantasy, Mark could stare at the shirtless Mr. Simmons as long as he liked. Puffing on his pipe, Mr. Simmons waved Mark over from across the street, shouting something about his hardy Bermuda grass. Simmons was so hirsute and frighteningly real, the scent of tobacco so resinous and sweet, that the fantasy began to buckle under its own weight, and Mark wouldn't allow himself to get any closer than the curb. Yet that was as close as he had to get before he felt unfaithful to Joe.

Not until the Fourth of July, while Peter and his parents were barbecuing in the backyard, did Mark have the house to himself. He assumed that Peter had long ago thrown Guy Joe into the trash, but to his amazement, he found the doll in the first place he looked: the cedar trunk. Peter had probably figured that, being so obvious, this was the last place Mark would look. Buried under the M-80s and baseball cards, Guy Joe lay in his cardboard box. Translucent patches of glue and nubs of lint covered his body, waxy crumbs clinging to his crotch. He looked derelict, bedraggled, smaller and paler than Mark remembered, like someone allowed into the sunlight after a long imprisonment.

Mark stared at Joe and shook his head; it was hard to believe this decrepit doll had once affected him. Driven by a force as strong as lust, Mark sat on his bed, took a deep breath, and tore off Guy Joe's arms and legs. The M-80s barely fit into the empty sockets; Mark had to force them with all his might, clamping the doll between his knees. Darkness was still an hour away, but already he could hear kids setting off the fireworks they'd bought at rickety stands outside the city: Mad Dancers, Whistling Piccolos, Freedom Cones. When Mark was done, the doll looked like a mad scientist's experiment gone wrong: half stunted man, half brown-eyed bomb.

Mark slammed the door behind him and strode to the middle of the parched front lawn. The smell of charcoal filled the air, along with staticky patriotic music from the Kerns' transistor radio. Fading rays of daylight glinted off parked cars and metal awnings, the peaks of the San Gabriels tipped in a molten glow. Everyone in the neighborhood seemed to be eating outdoors, splashing in plastic pools, waiting for night to fall so they could wave tiny flags and set off explosions in a noisy spasm of celebration. Mark fished a book of matches from his pocket and lit Joe's fuses one by one. The voices of his family drifted over the redwood fence, their chatter like a foreign language, and it occurred to Mark that he might have been born in a faraway country, adopted as a baby by the Kerns; maybe that was why the life his family took for granted was hard for him to understand. But he couldn't picture his place of birth, or remember its people, customs, clothes. Rearing back, he took aim at the sky, the heat of the fuses creeping toward his hand.

exterior
decoration

Standing at the living room window, Ray looked up from his morning coffee and saw that the garage door of the house across the street, which just yesterday had been a shade of beige, was now painted a sumptuous red. Ray froze mid-sip. He suspected that Cliff, still asleep in their bed, had sneaked out and done it in the middle of the night.

Ray had hidden the paint, the brushes, and the roller in various drawers and shelves around their house, but when inspiration struck, no matter how tired or stunned by medication, Clifford could sniff out latex paint with the tenacity of a police dog. Since they'd moved into the house, Cliff had painted their living room a color called Rainy Slate, and then, a few dissatisfied days later, a color called Old Parchment, and finally a pale blue called Fog, which made the walls seem moist and insubstantial. At first, Ray found it hard not to indulge Cliff in his aesthetic experiments; Cliff was a decorator after all, or had been before he went on disability, a man who loved to gaze at paint samples, their very names—Almond, Sand Castle, Jade Escape—transporting him like poetry. Eventually, however, Cliff's aesthetic grew aggressive, seeping beyond the confines of their house; the more Cliff resigned himself to the uncertainty of his health, the more intolerant he became when faced with the world's ugliness and disarray. "'Mere anarchy is loosed upon the world'!" he'd quote as they drove through the city. Or, more prosaically, he'd grouse about the graffiti on a bus bench, the bleak uniformity of a strip mall, or a bronze lump that passed for public sculpture. It might have been a side effect of the steroids, or the antidepressants, or the protease inhibitors, or any number of experimental drugs that were mingling in Clifford's bloodstream, but in recent months he seemed to believe that his acts of decoration would eventually change the world.

The first of these occurred at Christmas, when the poinsettias bunched on the Donahues' front steps had been mysteriously moved to a spot beneath their bay window and arranged in a perfect semicircle. A few weeks later, Peter and Mehee Hyun discovered that their old porch light had been replaced by a chrome fixture neither of them recalled installing. And only last month, while Ray was at work, Cliff had decided to repaint a cinder-block retaining wall two doors down the street. After Mr. Cabrillo, the wall's rightful owner, called to complain, Cliff justified the act by telling Ray that burnt sienna went better with ivy than the original yellow, which he called "acidic and hideous," as if the color were a personal affront.

"But it's not our wall," Ray had tried to explain.

"It faces our property."

"So does Bingo when he lies on the Cabrillos' front steps, but you wouldn't go over and dye his fur."

"I might," said Cliff, sprawled on the velveteen divan he'd bought at an estate sale. "He's getting a little gray around the muzzle."

"Clifford, you can't go around redecorating the world because this or that offends your taste."

"You say 'taste' as if it's superficial. But taste is a deep and instinctive drive for order, an essential part of who we are. And my taste, let's face it, is highly refined."

"Call it whatever you want. The point is, Mr. Cabrillo is pissed. I don't know about you, but I'd like to live here for a while before we get run out of the neighborhood on a rail." Thanks to Ray's promotion at the phone company, they had bought this house in the Silverlake Hills after spending four years in a cramped one-bedroom apartment. Their former downstairs neighbor, a portly man with darting eyes, woke them up at least once a week by knocking on their door and shouting, "I know you're doing aerobics. I know you're doing aerobics. You woke me up. I need to dream." Ray thought it was clear from the bleary state in which he opened the door that *he* was the one who'd been awakened, but Benton would pant and babble to himself, finally trying to barge into their apartment, though "barge" was too strong a word to describe his timid assault. Getting rid of Benton had been as easy as nudging a helium balloon back into the hallway and gently shutting the door behind it. In any case, Benton's early-morning visits highlighted their need to move into a larger, quieter place, especially after Cliff's T-cells had dropped below two hundred and the need for rest loomed in their future.

"Okay," Cliff had said at last. "You win. I'll apologize to Mr. Cabrillo about the wall."

"And . . . ?"

"Um, to Bingo, too?"

"You've got to repaint it."

Cliff sat up, folded his arms. "Not that awful yellow again. A man's got limits."

"Clifford, you will paint the wall whatever color Mr. Cabrillo wants it painted. It is not your decision. One does not get up in the middle of the night and decide to remodel a neighbor's property."

"You're enunciating," said Cliff. "I hate it when you enunciate."

"I'm enunciating because you do not seem to understand what has happened here. Decorating has ramifications!"

"That's what I've been trying to tell you all along! Taste affects everything!"

And now, as if the incident with the retaining wall hadn't been troublesome enough, Cliff had tried his hand at an even bigger canvas: the Heartleys' garage door. Ray gulped the tepid dregs of his coffee and recalled that Mr. and Mrs. Heartley opened the door by pushing a button inside the house, so it was possible they might get into their respective cars that morning and drive off to work without seeing it close behind them, conspicuous and crimson. It was seven A.M., and though Cliff needed his rest, especially after what must have been an industrious night, Ray decided to wake him and insist that he do whatever he could to restore the garage door, or at least compose a note of apology before the Heartleys returned from work.

No sooner had Ray entered the bedroom than Cliff stirred.

He'd been so unpredictable these days, so likely a candidate for scolding, that excuses seemed to bubble from his sleep. "It was too white," he mumbled, opening his eyes. His dry mouth crackled, lips as pale as Old Parchment. "It was bright as a damn klieg light. I could practically see the thing with my eyes closed. You want me to get a good night's sleep, don't you?" Ray gazed down at Cliff, a groggy man tangled in blankets, and could barely muster the wherewithal for a confrontation. He sat at the edge of the bed and smoothed Cliff's hair, flecked by telltale drops of red paint. Cliff propped his head in Ray's lap. His bare arm was veiny and lean, yet solid from steroids. "Don't you think it gives their house more character?" asked Cliff. "It's Chinese Red, a royal color."

"Oh, Cliff."

"What?"

Ray sighed. "It doesn't make any difference what I think. Or what you think. The Heartleys get to have it whatever color they want. This hit-and-run remodeling can't go on. It's . . . un-neighborly." Ray stopped himself from saying "insane," a word that might set Cliff off, make him worry that he was experiencing the early stages of AIDS dementia, something he feared even more than physical pain. It had happened before—once, after misplacing his car keys, Cliff began to question his sanity, convinced that everything he did and said seemed strange, his small blunders and lapses of memory destined to get worse and worse until he was finally mired in confusion, a young man abandoned by his once-refined senses. Ray reassured him that misplacing one's car keys fell within the range of acceptable mistakes, and that any perfectly rational person, taking so many medications, might be subject to bouts of odd behavior. But ever since Clifford began his tasteful reign of terror, Ray was beginning to wonder himself. Still, his lover's eloquence and sudden, unguarded enthusiasms made it hard for Ray to believe, at least for very long, that someone so vital could be losing his mind.

"I get so wired late at night," said Cliff. "Everything starts fluttering. You should hear what goes on in my head, little complaints that won't let go. Colors are off, proportions all wrong. After a certain hour, there's no peace until I get up and *do* something."

"Why don't you watch TV?"

"There's nothing on except infomercials, and two minutes into them I start thinking that I can't live without a fruit dehydrator or a Miracle Mop. It's dangerous. I have to hide my credit cards, but of course, then I know where they're hidden."

"You could wake me. We could talk."

"Do you have any idea how you look when you're asleep? You positively radiate the benefits of oblivion. I need you asleep for inspiration."

"You used to love to draw. Why don't you take up drawing?"

Cliff laughed, nuzzled Ray's leg. "I've taken up painting. It's more of a challenge."

"Right," said Ray. "For me."

The doorbell rang, and they looked at each other with apprehension. "Great," groaned Cliff. "Everything seems so different in the daylight. If the sun stayed out all night I'd be a much more responsible person." He kept his head firmly planted in Ray's lap, as if the weight of his cranium might keep Ray from rising to his feet.

Ray slipped free and took a deep breath. He had no idea how he was going to explain the situation to the Heartleys, and he hoped some halfway reasonable excuse might strike him before he reached the door. Ray would have to treat Vince Heartley with kid gloves, and not just because of the garage door. Shortly after Ray and Cliff had moved into the house, the Whittier earthquake shook the city, and the Heartleys had called an impromptu neighborhood meeting of what Vince had dubbed the Regional Alert Team. "RAT," said Cliff, "a fine acronym in a time of crisis." Ray insisted Cliff come along because he wanted the neighbors to get used to the fact that the two of them were a couple. And so Cliff squeezed into his best turtleneck and went.

Seated in the Heartleys' living room, Ray listened with what he hoped was ingratiating interest while Vince, barrel-chested and gravel-voiced, dragged out his collection of fire extinguishers, water purification tablets, and state-of-the-art flashlights, demonstrating them for the Cabrillos and the Hyuns and the Donahues, all of whom complimented Vince on his expertise. Cliff, on the other hand, peered around the room and took in every nuance of decor, reciting Yeats's line about anarchy whenever an aftershock rattled the house. The Cabrillos had brought Bingo, who growled and bared his teeth at every tremor. "Dogs can sense a quake right before it happens," said Hector Cabrillo, scratching the agitated rottweiler behind the ears. This came as unnerving news to Mehee and Peter Hyun, huddled together in the middle of the couch and watching the dog for signs of doom. "Our area may not have sustained much damage today," Vince announced to the traumatized neighbors, "but tomorrow could be a different story. Preparedness is the best safeguard against disaster. I know this for a fact, people. I've been in the National Guard, so me and adversity are old friends." Vince began to itemize the contents of his first-aid kit and, to Ray's mortification, Cliff interrupted by asking, "Are these the original window treatments? Or were they here when you bought the house?" Vince ignored Cliff and forged ahead with—Ray could almost see him think it—the more manly and important topic at hand. Delores, however, who had decorated the house herself, was charmed by Cliff's inquiry. She and Cliff whispered in a corner while Vince continued talking, and all his angry sidelong glances couldn't dampen their enthusiasm. Soon, the Cabrillos and the Hyuns and the Donahues lost interest in what Ray thought was Vince's unnecessarily gory lecture on triage; instead, they were eavesdropping on a whispered conversation about horizontal versus vertical blinds. "The thing with verticals," blurted Arthur Donahue, "is that you don't have to dust them." His observation met with nods of agreement and a pat on the back from his languid wife, Sherry, whose long pink fingernails betrayed her distaste for housework. Meanwhile, too proud to beg for his guests' attention, Vince unfurled streamers of surgical gauze and, with a somewhat desperate theatricality, wrapped himself in a glinting Mylar blanket.

Later that night, as they undressed for bed, Ray accused Cliff of disrupting the first (and only, as it turned out) meeting of RAT. "Couldn't you have at least *pretended* to listen to Vince? Don't you think there's a time to put interior decoration on the back burner?"

"What better time to discuss the ideal environment," said Cliff, "than when the earth is heaving herself to pieces? Besides, I think about death often enough as it is. 'I've been to the phlebotomist's,'" Cliff boomed in Vince's gravelly voice, "'so me and adversity are old friends.'" Cliff peeled off his turtleneck like an old, constricting skin. "Really, Ray, the neighbors were far more interested in miniblinds than they were in knowing how to stanch the blood flow from their carotid arteries. Delores Heartley wants to be my best friend, for God's sake, and Arthur was overjoyed to find another male with whom he can discuss the art of dusting without feeling that he's compromised his masculinity. If you want to be upset about something, I suggest you worry about how Sherry Donahue is going to dig herself out from under the rubble with those fingernails of hers. Besides," said Cliff, poking Ray's chest, "you're just jealous I was such a huge hit."

Ray grabbed Cliff's hand and pulled him close. He could feel Cliff's ribs, the force of Cliff's breath against his neck. What did an argument about social conduct mean in the scheme of things? So many of their arguments had come to seem ludicrous in the face of AIDS, which tended to give Ray the long view—especially tonight, given the shifting tectonic plates, the erosion of the coastline. Five years before, they'd had to negotiate safer sex and get used to being a sero-different couple. Now, without forethought or talk, their combined body heat did what only skin can do: burned away the differences between them. And so they had kissed, quickly stripping as tremors shook the house.

The doorbell rang at ever more impatient intervals, and Ray picked up his pace; he could picture Vince standing on the front steps, large and florid with pent-up resentment. Ray forced a benign smile and opened the door, wondering if he had enough cash on hand to pay for the damage.

The man and woman on the landing wore blue uniforms, silver badges glinting in the sun. They stood side by side, their posture perfect, like figures atop a police department wedding cake. "Good morning, sir," said the female officer. She adjusted her hat, and a strand of auburn hair fell across her forehead. "Mind if we ask you a few questions?"

"Not at all," said Ray. He peered into the street, wondering, with a flush of embarrassment, if everyone in the neighborhood would notice the squad car parked in front of their house, police code crackling from its radio. "Would you care to come in?"

The officers squared their shoulders and touched their guns, as if Ray had invited them for hors d'oeuvres and an ambush. They warily entered the living room, clearly trained to assess any environment at a glance—a talent not dissimilar to Cliff's. "The color's called Fog," Ray offered. "My partner picked it out." The officers looked at each other. Ray gestured toward the velveteen divan and asked if they'd care to sit down. "We'll stand," said the man.

"Whatever you'd like. Can I get you something to drink?" Ray heard the obsequious tone that crept into his voice whenever he dealt with authority figures or people in uniform. At work, he was all grinning compliance when it came to his superiors. At home, he treated the mail carrier like a visiting diplomat, offering her iced tea and moist towelettes when the weather turned hot. Ray's five siblings had shoplifted, cruised Hollywood Boulevard by the raucous carload, and routinely set fires in the Dumpster behind their apartment complex, while Ray was what his mother called a model citizen. She'd never grasped the fact that her son was homosexual, and so, when she pleaded with her other children to be more like him, they looked at her with pity and turned up their music. Despite the torment visited upon him by his siblings—"Brown-noser!" "Teacher's pet!"—Ray had always found that being a do-gooder had certain advantages, the most obvious being the way it kept him in people's good graces and allowed him to live in relative peace. Who in his right mind wanted trouble?

"Is that Vince?" Cliff chimed from the bedroom.

"No," said Ray. "It's someone else."

"I'm Officer Flores," said the woman. "And this is *my* partner, Officer Novakovich."

"How do you do," said Ray. He suddenly remembered that he'd thanked the highway patrolman who'd given him his last traffic ticket. Thanked him! "Any time," the cop had said, revving his cycle and speeding off.

"Do you happen to know anything about the garage door across the street, Mr. . . . ?"

"Praeger. The Heartleys' garage door?"

"That's correct," said Novakovich.

"It's red," said Ray, stalling for time. How could he implicate Cliff without getting him arrested?

Clifford's voice wafted from afar, faint yet emphatic. "It's *Chinese* Red."

"Your partner?" asked Flores. "Mind if we speak with him, too?"

"Sure. Let me get him. Will you excuse me a minute?"

"A minute," she said. "We need to fill out a preliminary investigation report, and we don't want to keep the victim waiting."

"The victim?"

"Mr. Heartley."

"Oh," said Ray. "Of course."

In the bedroom, Cliff was hopping on one foot and tugging his jeans on with such haste, Ray worried he might fall over. The blinds were still closed, and in the dim light, Clifford's eyes looked overly bright. "I can't believe it," he said. "This is simply unbelievable."

"What did you expect?" Ray grumbled, quickly trying to make the bed. Keeping things neat helped him think, and he needed a plan.

"I expected he'd be out of our lives for good."

"You . . . huh?" Ray stopped smoothing the sheet.

"Can he hear us doing aerobics from across town? I suppose his hearing is better than Bingo's."

Ray's heart began to race. "What are you talking about?"

"Benton. I'm talking about Benton. Isn't he at the door?" Cliff's battle with his jeans suddenly stopped. He stood in the dark, hair matted, jaw slack, his unbuckled belt hanging from the loops. It was as if all the hinges that held him together had suddenly swung loose. Ray yanked open the vertical blinds, half hoping he would turn from the window and see Cliff restored, not simply to the man he'd been, but to the man he'd been before they'd met, before his body succumbed to a virus, moment by moment, cell by cell. Cliff stood in a blaze of morning light. He blinked and breathed, wearing one of the crisp white shirts he used to wear when visiting a client, a shirt, Ray noticed, that now seemed much too big and officious.

"Sir," came a voice from the living room. "Mr. Praeger?"

"How will we ever get rid of him? Will we have to move again, Ray? Is there enough paint for our new rooms?" Cliff's voice trembled though his eyes were dry.

Ray wanted to whisper something comforting, but he heard himself say, "Stop it. You're scaring me." He lunged toward Cliff, hugging him so hard it startled them both.

"Mr. Praeger, is everything okay?"

"No," shouted Ray. "Everything is not okay. Give us a minute, for Christ's sake."

Outside, static erupted from the police radio, abrasive as sandpaper. Over Cliff's shoulder, through the open blinds, Ray saw Vince and Delores peering into the street from a window above the garage. The Donahues and the Hyuns and the Cabrillos had gathered around the police car. They talked and nodded, thoroughly delighted, Ray was sure, that an otherwise boring day had been disrupted. Above the heads of his neighbors, as far as Ray could see, houses of every size and color studded the hills—temporary shelter, according to Vince, till the big one hits.

"Mr. Praeger," said Officer Novakovich, "your minute is up. We'd like both of you to step out here ASAP. This is not some little Halloween prank we're dealing with. If we find that either you or your . . . friend is in any way responsible, and if the damages exceed five grand, we're looking at a felony."

"Will you go deal with him?" pleaded Cliff. "I can't handle Benton, not this morning. You always tell me how easy it is to push him back into the hallway and shut the door like nothing happened. You say he's light as a helium balloon. But that's the thing about being crazy, Ray; it makes you lighter, not heavier. Sooner or later your feet leave the ground. And there's so much to do and say before you're gone. That's why Benton talks to himself. That's why he's always out of breath." Cliff stepped free of Ray's embrace. "That's why I'm never able to sleep." He rested a hand on Ray's shoulder, urged him back to the waiting world.

But Ray, flooded by a strange calm, refused to move. At least not yet. Despite Cliff's glassy bewildered eyes, his face looked handsome, chiseled down to the necessary flesh. It would be months before Cliff died of spinal meningitis, delirious from a morphine drip, ripping the IV from his wrist and howling because of how much it hurt, cursing the nurses who ran into the room, calling Ray by the wrong name. For the moment, though, Ray Praeger almost believed that if the two of them stayed exactly where they were, if they didn't say another word, the day might never deepen into evening, their troubles might remain at bay, and Ray could linger with the man he loved, without regret or consequence.

graphology

Libby Arenson tried to concentrate on the six o'clock news while her husband jogged laps through their living room, dining room, kitchen, and foyer. Carl Arenson weighed almost two hundred pounds, though exercise kept him massive rather than fat, and when his wife watched him bounding by, he brought to mind, with his heavy footfalls and the bulky musculature of his upper back, a stampeding bison. As he swerved around the furniture, dressed in a T-shirt and sweat pants, perspiration darkened his armpits and glistened through his thinning hair. He panted harder with every lap, and the harder he panted, the more vividly she recalled how it felt to lie naked beneath him, the two of them arching, out of breath.

She shifted on the living room sofa, turned up the volume on the weather report. Clouds swirled over a satellite map of Southern California and sputtered drops of animated rain, the real thing just then beginning to pelt the awnings and roof. Mrs. Arenson had long ago grown accustomed to Carl's habit of exercising indoors during bouts of bad weather, and now the rain glazing the flagstone patio and the clockwork of her husband's jogging intensified her sense of shelter. Libby and Carl had lived together for thirty years.

The top story that night involved a team of French scientists who'd successfully cloned a mouse. The original and its duplicate were shown on a sea of shredded newspaper. The sight of them, jittery and white, made Mrs. Arenson twist her wedding ring around her finger; life's assumptions were up for grabs. Did they grow the clone in a petri dish? Did the cells turn into a rodent overnight? She called for Carl, a professor of applied science at UCLA, to come quickly. There she sat in a comfortable room, remote control at her disposal, and something as small as a mouse's cell threw everything she knew for a loop. Not until halfway through a commercial for . . . what *was* it for, anyway? There were so many quick cuts she couldn't tell—did she realize that Carl had missed the story. On her way to the kitchen, she noticed the imprints of his running shoes, fresh spoor, stamped into the carpet. She called for him once more, and when he didn't answer, she figured he's gone upstairs to shower and change for dinner.

The second hand of the old kitchen wall clock faintly groaned as it labored upward, then fell silent as it ticked downhill. A pot of rice began to boil over on the stove, froth hissing as it struck the flame. Mrs. Arenson turned off the gas and set the pot on a back burner, still hearing what she at first mistook for the familiar noises of the kitchen. Days later, when she replayed this moment, she couldn't help but wonder at how stubbornly she'd gone about her evening routine, unwilling to hear a sound that, in retrospect, was far more eerie and urgent than those she usually noticed. Perhaps to drown it out, she'd hummed a song that had been in her head since the clock radio woke her that morning. She rummaged through the freezer till she found the broccoli in cheese sauce, cool fog wafting toward her face. As she read the microwave directions, she heard a rasping and saw, out of the corner of her eye, a man slumped on the floor of the foyer. The overhead fixture cast stripes of light across the floral wallpaper, and it was this camouflaging effect she would later blame for not immediately registering the fact that the man was Carl, his body so imploded from pain that whatever had made him robust and mobile no longer belonged to him. Her stomach clenched at the sight of this stranger. She was about to shout for Carl to call the police, but when she heard herself say his name, it was shrill with recognition and pity.

Carl's mouth, as she swooped close, opened wide, and she understood that the air around him had turned solid. She, too, found herself struggling to breathe. Kneeling on the terra-cotta tiles, she cupped his head in her hands, still icy from the freezer. His cheeks, she discovered, were unusually cool, the heat of his temples slipping through her fingers. Mr. and Mrs. Arenson looked at each other, and there passed between them a gust of surprise—no less terrible because it was shared—at how quickly the two of them had grown cold. His eyes, she saw, were flaring with reflected light, but the man who gazed through them was receding into some solitary inner distance, his every need irretrievable: to breathe, or speak, or reach for his wife.

*   *   *

A few days after her husband's burial, as she undressed for bed, Mrs. Arenson heard the voices of her son and his fiancée talking downstairs. Cinching her bathrobe, she crept to the landing, where light from the foyer glowed in the stairwell. That morning, Josh had promised to stay with his mother until she adjusted to . . . he was about to say something like "Dad's death," but was stopped from finishing his sentence by the overwrought sense of tact that tended to get the better of him in a crisis. His protectiveness toward his mother, his ready euphemisms—"passing" instead of "death," "service" instead of "funeral"—only added to the unreality of Mrs. Arenson's bleary days and sleepless nights. Not to mention the fact that Josh, his woolly hair thinning, shoulders squared as he measured every word, looked disconcertingly like his father. As she leaned over the banister, eavesdropping, she found herself wishing that Josh and his fiancée would fly back home and leave her with the loneliness that having houseguests only postponed.

"This one," Josh was saying, "is almost like a face."

"Oh, right." Deena laughed. "If you were on drugs."

"No, really," he persisted. "Look."

Silence as Deena no doubt leaned forward to examine one of the hundreds of flowers Carl had been in the process of re-painting. Nearly five years ago, Mrs. Arenson had casually re-marked that the wallpaper in the foyer, with its repetition of a frail violet, now seemed to her too quaint and old-ladyish. And so Carl had begun to repaint them one by one. Some he merely recolored: "Is a yellow violet still a violet?" he'd once asked her from the top rung of a stepladder, a sable brush gripped in his fist. Others he'd transformed into knobby roses and radiant daisies. Mr. Arenson averaged six or so flowers a month. Bifocals perched on the tip of his nose, he'd dab at the wall with great concentration, using a scrap of cardboard as his palette. Eventually, he graduated from what he jokingly called "your garden-variety flower" to more exotic blossoms: hybiscus, chrysanthemums, dahlias. These were followed by gaudy, ponderous flora that sprang directly, Mrs. Arenson figured, from an imagination that applied science and school administration did little to stimulate.

"What do you think got into him?" asked Deena.

"I guess it was cheaper than buying new wallpaper."

"That's very insightful for a psychotherapist," teased Deena. "But it doesn't do much to explain his motivation. I mean, you have to admit it's a little weird, for all its charm."

"No," said Josh. "I don't have to admit anything of the sort. I think . . . when a man like my father, an average man, does something . . . out of the ordinary, he . . ."

The more Josh faltered, the more tightly Mrs. Arenson gripped the banister, waiting for some remark that might explain the husband whom, until earlier that night, she thought she knew. She fought the urge to call for Josh and Deena to come and look at what she'd discovered in Carl's briefcase, to help her decipher the crimped hieroglyphics. Maybe Josh had had experience with such matters in his practice, though her son was the last person she'd dare to ask. She leaned away from the rising light, told herself that no one must know.

Josh said, "You're being . . ."

"You're right, babe. I'm sorry. It's just that, in a house as suburban as this, the slightest eccentricity gets magnified."

Josh admitted that he'd always found his father's pastime a little strange. "Dad was big on order and decorum. And then this! He got such a kick out of showing the wallpaper to guests, which he'd do the moment they walked in the door. Mom would throw up her hands and groan, 'Carl, please. Not the hothouse!'"

Mrs. Arenson remembered with fresh embarrassment how Paul Nordon, one of Carl's colleagues, had squinted at the flowers, his silence a not-so-subtle judgment. Regardless, Carl continued to point out each bloom with boyish glee, waiting till Nordon finally gave in and grunted with polite appreciation. It sometimes seemed as if the papered walls were a gauntlet visitors had to pass through in order to earn the niceties of socializing: a seat, a drink, a bowl of salted nuts. Although the foyer was a place of countless reunions and partings, of sentiment's formalities, once Carl began to fuss with the wallpaper, it became a room Mrs. Arenson couldn't quite reconcile with the rest of her house, nor with what the years had taught her about her husband's character. Carl's ability to recite the periodic table or explain particle theory to a layperson had been the very thing about him she'd initially found attractive, certain it testified to a pragmatism that matched her own. But the list she'd discovered among her husband's papers, penned in a tiny, obsessive script, had obliterated in an instant her deepest reserves of certainty. And now the flowers, or his impulse to paint them, seemed to play some part.

Earlier that night, while Josh and Deena had noisily prepared dinner downstairs, Mrs. Arenson sat on Carl's side of the bed, his briefcase propped on her lap. She'd already searched through his nightstand and desk drawers for the documents she'd need in order to settle the estate, and for the utility bills she'd have to pay, though she couldn't help but think that a disconnected phone might not be so bad—all those kind but awkward condolences cut off at the source. It took only a few tries to find the right combination to the briefcase (3, 2, 1; Carl was so logical!), the latches springing open with a snap. Inside, she found his bifocals, a few complimentary textbooks addressed to Professor Arenson, memos from Paul Nordon about next semester's lab budget, and a small stack of bluebooks, which the university provided for midterms. She read the compliments Carl had scrawled in the margins—*"Good point"*; *"Clear and concise"*—as well as remarks that betrayed his impatience with shoddy scholarship. She thought how odd it was going to be for the students to have their tests returned, an inheritance of notations.

At the bottom of the stack lay a bluebook marked "Instructor Only," which Mrs. Arenson took to be the key to the midterm's essay and multiple-choice questions. Instead, she flipped it open to find page after page of stuttering numbers and mysterious acronyms she at first mistook for some lengthy, complex formula. The ballpoint had been pressed into the paper with great force, leaving impressions on the pages beneath, and before she fully grasped what she was seeing, Mrs. Arenson tensed at the sight of the handwriting, a penmanship so stiff and precise, she suspected the marks had hurt the hand that made them.

Each entry yielded a male name—Casey, Philip, Mike— none of which appeared to belong to Carl's students. These were followed by abbreviations for hair and eye color: Bl., brn., blk. There were telephone numbers, estimates of weight and age, and what Mrs. Arenson concluded, after several alarming appraisals, had to be the measurement of each man's penis, followed by adjectives such as "thick" or "uncut." A number of descriptions—*"Portwine birthmark," "Walks with limp"*—were spelled out unmistakably. Carl seemed to have not only noticed but doted upon the way each of these bodies deviated from perfection, a fact even more frightening to Mrs. Arenson than the possibility that her husband had pursued some unattainable male ideal. His desire for men either exempted her from failure (how could she give him something she wasn't?), or meant that she had failed completely, driving him to men. She recalled with momentary relief how Carl had made love while staring at her with the same intensity that claimed him when he painted, but then she wondered if he'd found it possible to fantasize about men with his eyes wide open. Her hands shook, her throat closed. Mrs. Arenson peered down at the pages and felt as though she were falling headlong into the well of her husband's briefcase. When Deena yelled up to ask where she kept the placemats, she found herself saying in a stricken voice, "I don't understand what you're asking."

"Never mind, Mom," shouted Josh. "They were right in front of us the whole time."

Dr. Fernandez swabbed the inside of Mrs. Arenson's mouth, cupping her chin in his palm, his touch a reminder of the tenderness she'd have to do without. "I'm not sure why you're insisting on this, Libby" he said, labeling the sample to be sent to the lab. She assured him she had her reasons, and the doctor, who had treated both her and Carl since they were married, didn't persist. "Use protection," he warned her, averting his eyes. Libby slid off the examination table, the sheet of clean paper crinkling beneath her, and grabbed her handbag.

A few days later she received the call. Her relief at the results was instantly replaced by a fretful investigation of her husband's pockets, his phone and date books, the folders in his filing cabinet. Josh and Deena had been gone almost a week—the house was hers at last—but Mrs. Arenson couldn't shake the expectation that every time she turned a corner or opened a door, she'd come across some sign of Carl: the spread pulled back on his side of the bed, a dish he'd left to soak in the sink. This reflex at first saddened, then angered her. She retrieved the bluebook from her husband's briefcase, ran her finger down the page, and stopped at a twenty-four-year-old brunet. Her choice was more or less arbitrary, though her wish to ask questions was as strong as lust. Dialing the boy's number, she resolved not to let herself sound aggrieved or vindictive, the put-upon wife. She would remain calm enough to coax from— she had to double-check the name—to coax from Casey what insight she could. Although Libby had taken the AIDS test days ago, she swore she could still sense the rough spot in her mouth where cells had been scraped away, and she probed it now with her tongue. While daylight dimmed in the windows, she paced back and forth and listened to the ringing on the other end of the line. Her heart was racing, yet she felt, as Carl must have, that she had an advantage; she knew the boy she was calling by name, knew his intimate, distinguishing features, knew more about him than he about her. She managed "Hello," when Casey answered. She stammered, "This is very awkward." But when a voice, close to her ear, asked, "Who is this?" Mrs. Arenson couldn't speak.

Approaching the glass doors of the Glendale Library, Mrs. Arenson glanced from side to side, worried she'd run into someone she knew. Hidden by a pair of sunglasses, her eyes were swollen from sleeplessness; night after night, she was startled from dreams she could never quite remember. She had tried Ativan, then Ativan and warm milk, then Ativan and brandy, finally sleeping with the T-shirt Carl had worn the night he died, the sour traces of her husband's sweat as welcome and quelling as lungfuls of ether. But the comfort never lasted for long; clinging to a hank of fabric (could she ever bring herself to wash it?) made their bed feel desolate, empty. And who was she mourning anyway? A stranger who went by Carl's name?

Although she'd once worked as a research assistant for Jacob Trevor, her sophomore history professor, Mrs. Arenson hadn't stepped inside a library for years. All around her, people searched through the stacks or thumbed through *Books in Print*. She approached a computer terminal and told herself she would have to live with whatever she discovered about her husband's secret life, if she discovered anything at all. Libby found herself so mystified by the task ahead, she might as well have lived in a flat, inexplicable world, ready to consult a sibyl or interpret the stars.

She typed in her keyword and hit Find, remembering with a swift, involuntary clarity one of the dreams from which she'd recently awakened: she'd been back in college, doing research for Professor Trevor on human cloning, and the drawer of the card catalogue kept coming toward her, inch after indexed inch. She'd spent what seemed like hours of sluggish dream time searching through a foreign alphabet, getting nowhere, certain Trevor would be furious at her incompetence. And so it was with especially dense apprehension that she scrolled through the list of books on the screen, wondering if her dream had been some sort of portent. Libby Arenson was not by nature a superstitious woman—she had never looked for, or considered anything in retrospect to be, a portent—and when she finally located the library's dozen or so books on graphology, she could almost hear Carl chide her for resorting to a pseudoscience.

The librarian glanced at the titles as she swiped the books across a scanner. "Idle curiosity," explained Mrs. Arenson. "My interests are usually more . . . sophisticated." She handed over her ancient library card, frayed at the edges.

"Mrs. Arenson," whispered the librarian, reading the card, "you don't have to be embarrassed with me. A friend of mine is really into this handwriting stuff. If I so much as sign a Master-Card receipt in front of her, she tells me something about myself I don't want to know. 'Nora,' she'll say, 'the tail on that A shows me you're awfully impulsive. You might try reining yourself in a little.'" Tall and long-limbed, Nora leaned confidingly toward Mrs. Arenson. "I mean, if I'm buying lunch, I figure I'm entitled to stay blissfully ignorant about my character flaws."

Libby folded her arms. "Your friend actually believes there's some validity in handwriting analysis?" *My God,* she thought, *I sound exactly like Carl.* It was one of those moments (lately, there were many) in which she found herself inhabited by her husband's professorial gestures, or heard his skeptical tone in her voice. If only she could recall him from a wistful distance, but ever since his death, she felt his traits burning her calories, moving her muscles, thriving inside her.

"And I suppose you think this is all a bunch of nonsense?" asked Nora, smiling wryly and holding up three volumes on graphology.

"I keep an open mind," said Libby, struck by just how ungraspable widowhood had turned out to be. She slipped her library card back into her wallet and—where on earth was her self-control?—began to cry.

The librarian's smile swiftly faded. "Are you all right?"

Libby tried to wave away the need for concern, but she started coughing and couldn't stop.

"Do you need to sit down?"

Libby pointed toward a water cooler she could see through the window of a back office.

Nora signaled to a young man, who replaced her at the checkout desk. She tucked Mrs. Arenson's books under her arm and led the way. Once inside the office, Nora offered water, pulled out a chair, and pressed a Kleenex into Libby's palm. Libby yielded to the librarian's ministrations, realizing it would take teamwork to stifle her crying. All the weeks she'd spent trying to suspend judgment about her husband, hoping to keep the truth at bay, had finally backfired. Slumped in the chair, trying to catch her breath, she revisited several of her most preposterous rationalizations, including one about Carl perhaps conducting an anatomical study of the urban male, a scenario she had been desperate enough to invent but not fool-ish enough to believe. As Libby wiped her eyes, she gazed through the glass window overlooking the main desk and watched several people passing by with books, books that would make them—or so she imagined—happier, wiser, more alive. She inhaled deeply and blew her nose. "I hate my hus-band," she announced. Her vehemence could have lit up a city. It felt so good, she said it again.

"The moment you're done crying," said Nora, "I'm going to ask you why. But for now I think you should let it all out."

Encouragement to weep as long and hard as she wanted had the effect of instantly drying Mrs. Arenson's tears. "You're very kind," she said to the librarian, wadding the Kleenex into a damp ball and eyeing the room for a wastebasket.

"I'm nosy, is what it is," said Nora, pointing to a trash can beneath the desk. "But I'll take any compliment, accurate or not."

"I bet you've never had to deal with a grown woman crying in line."

Nora laughed and shook her head. "You don't know the half of it, Mrs. Arenson . . ."

"It's Libby, please."

"I've seen everything, Libby. Teenagers humping in the reserve shelves. A regular patron who claims that extraterrestrials are sending him messages through microfilm. Once I even found a dead canary on the book cart—in a Baggie, thank God. You're a day at the beach, comparatively speaking."

Libby took a sip of water.

"So, why?" asked Nora.

"Why what?"

"Your husband. You were saying you hate him."

Libby stared at Nora. She loved her husband. What could have possessed the librarian to say such a thing? Then it was over, the brief, cleansing respite that sometimes follows sobbing. Libby reached into her purse and pulled out the bluebook. Maybe it was the librarian's garrulousness, or the muted room, or the view of people searching through books and dredging facts into the light—Libby decided then and there that Nora would be the first person, besides herself, to see the evidence of her husband's infidelity. Despite her anger, she felt somehow more loyal showing the list to a stranger rather than someone Carl had known. "Suppose you found this in your husband's things." she asked Nora. "What would you think?"

Nora took the bluebook and slowly turned the pages, at a loss for what to say. She towered over Mrs. Arenson, who looked up from her chair and watched Nora's face. Puzzlement crimping the brow. Unease around the mouth. It was almost as if Libby were reliving the night she'd opened Carl's briefcase, standing outside herself and watching her own incredulous expressions.

"I see," said Nora. "I'm sorry." She leaned against the edge of the table, looked Libby in the eyes. "Are you going to confront him?"

"Oh, there's . . . Carl died of a heart attack last month. I found this a couple of days later. Ever since then, I've come to doubt everything I'm able to remember about him, about us. Everything. I'm trying to find out whatever I can." She pointed to the books she'd withdrawn. "There's no one to ask, no other way to know."

In a carrel at the east end of the library, bluebook lying on the desk before her, Libby Arenson began a careful examination of the stems and loops and crossbars of her husband's handwriting. It soothed her to view the words as abstractions, free of meaning. She recalled an art history class in which the teacher had analyzed Delacroix's *Liberty Leading the People* as a series of formal lines and shapes, barely mentioning the bloody revolution of 1830. This had been the class in which Libby first noticed Carl. She'd found herself gazing across the aisle as changing light from a carousel of slides bathed her classmate's upturned face. How intently he had taken notes, the confines of a wooden desk chair accentuating his bulky male body. He was one of the few students who dressed for school; the creases in his pants were sharp, the lenses of his wire-rimmed glasses glinted in the lecture hall's gloom. It was a wonder she'd passed the course, given the amount of time she spent staring, wondering who he was and what he was like. Thanks to her persistence, they eventually met, and when they finally knew each other well enough to study together for the art history exam, Libby discovered that, instead of being a record of Carl's sensitive aesthetic impressions, his notebook contained only those dates and names and details that might show up on the test. If she had been disappointed, the feeling was soon overpowered by the soapy scent and reticent voice of the boy sitting beside her on the lawn of the commons, sharing his fastidious notes, an event that seemed, in memory at least, as epic as a Delacroix.

Nora touched Libby's shoulder and handed her a copy of *Revelations in Handwriting.* "According to my friend," she whispered, "this book is the best of the bunch." Nora smiled uncertainly. She wished Libby luck and returned to her post at the checkout desk. Libby squinted at the small print on the cover. She reached into her purse and realized she'd brought Carl's bifocals instead of her own, but when she slipped them on, she discovered their prescriptions were practically the same. "Learn what your handwriting says about you," read the small print on the cover, and, more promisingly, "See others as they really are." Relying on a book to give her insight into a man she'd lived with for over thirty years suddenly seemed like an admission of defeat. How could her own powers of observation have failed her all this time? Which was worse, to question who her husband was, or to question her own perceptions?

Libby's research skills were rusty, but she scanned the index—"Scroll," "Signature," "Space between words"—and decided to focus on the slant of Carl's handwriting, which leaned neither right nor left, but tended to move up and down on a vertical axis. According to the author, this style suggested "a certain rigidity of character" and, depending on the pressure, could also indicate "the rather unsavory trait of arrogance." Libby noted the inky depressions left by the pen, and considered how opinionated her husband had been when it came to the virtues of science and the superiority of the scientific method. Still, he was genuinely enthusiastic when discussing such matters; you would no more accuse Carl of being arrogant than you would a kid explaining his science project. Besides, with some people, men especially, it was hard to distinguish between cockiness and conviction.

As for "a certain rigidity of character," she as much as Carl had been a creature of routine. As a couple, they'd worked at achieving a circumscribed life, with its unvarying orbit of errands and meals and family outings. This predictability seemed to agree with Josh, who had inherited his father's love of logic, and who, unlike other, more rebellious children, rarely balked at the order imposed by his parents. Mrs. Arenson thought it absurd when Sheila, one of her few single friends ("Single *by choice*," Sheila would stress), once proclaimed, "Married people live so safely." As far as Libby was concerned, there was no safety when it came to love; the more one loved the more one risked—an elegant and frightening equation. She certainly didn't need to be told that a house in a good neighborhood and a joint bank account couldn't do a thing to spare her from loss. In fact, Libby thought that good luck, like bad luck, was something that *befell* her, a phenomenon she often had to prod herself to enjoy, since she hadn't necessarily earned or deserved it.

Mrs. Arenson looked up from the desk and saw a stand of

birch trees rising beyond the carrel's slim window. There had been nearly a month of uninterrupted rain, and now a tentative light filtered through the branches, mottling the lawn where people sprawled to read or talk. A shirtless boy had fallen asleep in a patch of sun, a book propped open on his pale chest. Even in sleep, his contemplative expression made it seem as if knowledge seeped into his skin, the book rising and falling with his breath.

When Libby glanced back at the desk, she saw her husband's cursive as though for the first time, observing something about it that no book on handwriting analysis could quite describe—a brittle vigilance, the vertical strokes firmly planted, like fence posts meant to resist the wind. It occurred to her that, if the penmanship of this compromising document were tighter and more guarded than his usual handwriting, it would be even less likely to yield revelations. She'd expected to find some visual evidence of an insecurity (withered i's?) for which his meetings with men were the compensation, or a hint of some unspoken childhood trauma (separated letters?) which had driven him, in a kind of helpless brinkmanship, to risk in adulthood those things he loved most. But after staring at his notes for almost an hour, she began to think that his guardedness, his success at living a parallel life, *was* the revelation she'd been seeking.

Carl was insatiable, that much was clear from the dozens of names. A need that required such variety to be satisfied was beyond Mrs. Arenson's comprehension. Her own life had been guided by the wish to find one, just one man with whom she could live happily and long. A sweet, singular devotion was the stuff of songs and movies and books, and she'd pursued it both before and after marriage. Although she had little to compare it with, sex with Carl had been tender and energetic, and this made temptation easy to ignore. Once, Paul Nordon kissed her in the hallway at a New Year's Eve party, his tongue darting into her mouth. Sudden lust caused him to lose his balance, and Libby had to help the poor teetering man to a nearby bedroom where he collapsed amid a pile of coats. Buzzing from a few glasses of champagne, flattered by his sloppy pass, she'd flirted with the urge to fall on top of Paul—until he patted his groin and slurred, "Put 'er here, honey bunch." "Honey bunch": what a dusty, ridiculous endearment! To Paul's chagrin, she'd laughed out loud, and the spell was broken, replaced by sober reasons to leave.

The boy on the lawn awakened, light finding the cleft of his chest, the creases in his young stomach, and Libby saw him as Carl might: someone to want. If her husband's thoughts and gestures could haunt her, why not his longing? She continued to stare through the window as the boy reached around to brush away blades of grass from his back. The effort stretched his torso, an untanned sliver of hip showing above his belt. The boy's book fell open on the lawn, and he picked it up, sinew moving beneath his forearms as he turned the pages, searching for his place. And when the boy stood up, buttoned his shirt, and walked away, Libby strained to see him through Carl's lenses. Her body, perched on the lip of the chair, had tensed with regret, a regret out of all proportion to the boy's departure.

Mrs. Arenson distracted herself for a while by gazing at famous signatures. Albert Einstein's, practically flat, showed "several compressed arcades and garlands." Tchaikovsky's was all jagged peaks and precipitous dips. The strokes of Oscar Wilde's signature thinned out at various points, a mannerism the graphologist saw as a sure sign of "irreconcilable conflict, a man about whom two acquaintances would offer vastly different impressions." Mrs. Arenson, however, suspected that the irregularities of a quill, or some other Victorian writing instrument, offered a far more likely explanation.

The strain of reading through the wrong glasses caused the pages to blur, the surface of the little desk veering away at odd angles. Libby closed *Revelations in Handwriting* and removed the bifocals, slipping them, along with Carl's bluebook, into her handbag. She trudged through the library's high-ceilinged main room, past the man who sat at the information desk, in front of which a line had formed. She went by the checkout desk, but Nora was nowhere to be seen. The library's glass doors swung open to a concrete plaza, where she spotted Nora on a bench, smoking a cigarette and gesturing to Libby to come and sit beside her. Libby obliged and, before she could stop herself, asked Nora for a smoke. "Any luck?" asked Nora, holding out a lighter. The flint sputtered a few times before it finally caught, and when Libby took a drag, her first since college, her lungs burned in a bracing inhalation. "Pointless," said Libby. "The whole idea was a waste of time." She tapped the ashes, remembering how worldly she'd felt when complaining with Sherry back in college, the two of them disgusted by a wrong that only the taste of tobacco could right. Cars circled the library's parking lot, the drivers seaching for an empty space. A parade of teenagers walking home from high school made a show of being coupled, plunging a hand in each other's pockets or draping an arm around their partner's neck, easy, raglike entanglements.

Nora asked, "Where are your books?"

"I decided to leave them inside."

"After all that?"

"After all that." Mrs. Arenson's limbs grew leaden, the plaza turning silvery and indistinct. The effects of nicotine offered a welcome taste of the oblivion she'd missed during her sleepless nights. Tossing in the dark, Libby had found herself guessing again and again at Carl's last thought. She imagined a star exploding inside his chest, its heat and debris radiating down his left arm, flaring into his jaw, and she became her husband, looking up at herself from the cold floor of the foyer and trying to explain, in this last protracted second, why he'd led a hidden life. He (she) wordlessly reassured the woman who held his head and hovered above him, her shocked face dissipating, its atoms snuffed like candles.

Mrs. Arenson heard Nora ask something about Carl—she recognized the gentle inflection of someone hoping not to overstep her bounds—and realized she didn't know much more about him than she had back in her art history class: a shadowy figure intent on his notes, a vessel for speculation. Now, Mrs. Arenson felt toward Carl a version of that original love, or, if it wasn't love exactly, then the wish to love him, tempered by questions.

"I keep thinking I'll find more clues," she told Nora, "something that might explain who he was, who I was to him. I'm the same person I've always been, with the same son, the same house. . . ."

"It's awful," said Nora, "those times when you can't even recognize your life. There must be books about women who've gone through something similar. If you want, I could . . ."

"No," she said. "But thanks."

"What will you do now?" asked Nora.

Libby sighed a cloud of smoke.

*   *   *

When driving home that afternoon, Mrs. Arenson noticed the cloudless sky, every house and tree and car made vivid by unstinting light. When she was a girl, fresh weather had stirred in her an almost physical awareness of time, a vastness in the midst of which Libby had once been unafraid. As she pulled into her driveway, it occurred to her that she hadn't thought about Carl for several minutes. Maybe things were about to change, to clarify like the air. She unlocked the front door and stepped into the foyer. All around her hovered the flowers that—Josh was right—resembled faces: inscrutable, painted by hand, no two alike. And once again she began to imagine her husband's encounters with other men.

between the sheets

So the guy who draws my blood—what do you call them? A blood-drawer?—tells me I'm his last needle stick of the day.

I say, "Nobody's ever called me a needle stick before."

"Make a fist," he says, inspecting the crook of my arm where a blue vein rises to the surface of my skin. I can't quite grasp that he's going to jab it, the syringe half hidden on a tray behind his back. I used to know why veins are blue, but I forgot it long ago, like most explanations.

"After I've drained you dry," he says, looking me in the eye to make sure I know he's joking, "I'm off to the mall." When he lowers his head, I see that his hair is thinning at the crown, and I guess he's maybe thirty, a few years older than me.

Fear makes my mouth taste metallic. The sounds in the

room—air streaming through an overhead vent, the wheels of his chair on linoleum—are louder than they should be. I look away as he swabs my skin, feeling the icy kiss of antiseptic.

"You okay?" he asks.

"Fine," I say, but it doesn't sound convincing.

"Anyway," he says, "my mother bought me a set of new sheets, and I'm going to the mall to return them. I've been sleeping on flowered sheets—really pretty, like a watercolor garden—and last week she comes over to my apartment, plops herself down on the couch and says, 'Teddy, we have to talk. Now, don't get defensive, but the one thing I truly wish is that—'

"'Mom,' I say. 'You know I'm never going to get married or give you grandchildren. We had this discussion years ago.'

"'Who said anything about grandchildren? I've given up on grandchildren. As far as I'm concerned, you can make love with whomever or whatever you want. Far be it from me to oppress you with my hopes. What I was going to say is that I wish you'd let me buy you some sheets that are a little less . . . feminine.'"

I ask if she was joking.

"No way! I just stare at her from the other end of the couch and say, 'You might recall that your husband, my father, also sleeps on flowered sheets, and that hasn't raised any serious doubts about his manhood. And what about Denny?' That's my older brother. 'He sleeps on flowered sheets, too, and according to Lisa, Denny has to shave twice a day.'"

The needle is nothing. The needle is a fleabite. But when I look down, blood is streaming into the vial. I haven't seen that much of my own blood since my last HIV test, the red so bright and alarming, you could use it to paint a stop sign. It's probably my imagination, but deep inside I feel a lack, something vital sucked away. I close my eyes and Teddy keeps talking.

"'But Teddy,' says my mother, 'those flowered sheets were bought by women.'"

"'And that makes it different? Listen to yourself, Mother!' I'm pacing at this point, flailing my arms. 'You're being absurd. I mean, say Lisa bought Dad a pair of lace panties, would his wearing them be okay with you because they were bought by a woman?'"

"'Oh, Teddy,' she says. 'Please don't put that picture in my head.' She gets all flustered and tugs at her sleeves. 'Besides, it's too late: I've already bought them. The sheets, I mean.' She reaches into her purse—it's as big as a feedbag—and pulls out a package wrapped in clear plastic. 'Just slip them on the bed, dear, that's all I'm asking. They're pure cotton, two hundred threads per inch.'"

The tourniquet hurts, but I'd rather feel it than the loss of blood. I ask Teddy what these masculine sheets look like.

"They look like denim, and what could be more queer than a denim bed? It's so Village People. But Mother nudges me into the bedroom and insists on helping me change the sheets, practically shredding the old ones in her zeal to strip the bed, dumping them onto the floor like so much floral junk. To get me into the spirit, she says, 'Make the corners tight, mister! I want to be able to bounce a dime off that topsheet!' It was so weird to have my mother in my bedroom, barking orders like a drill sergeant. I mean, I haven't had a man in months, but suddenly the room smells ripe with sex. I'm on my knees, stretching fitted elastic over one corner of the mattress when something occurs to me. 'Mother', I ask. 'How did you know what size to get?'

"She strokes her chin. 'I'm a very good guesser.'"

"'Plus you must have done some snooping.' I keep the door to my bedroom closed whenever she's over, so how else would she know what kind of sheets I sleep on, or whether my bed was a full or a twin, a queen or a king? Anyway, she stands back and folds her arms. 'Well, I have to hand it to myself,' she says. 'I looked through more sheets than you'd need in a lifetime—Calvin's and Wamsutta's and an entire sale table full of dreadful polyester blends—and these are ideal. Try them out for me, Teddy.'

"When I balk, she calls me a party pooper."

"And?" I ask.

"I lie on my back. I lie on my side. I plump the pillow. Finally, I turn onto my stomach and stroke the sheets like I'm swimming through them. Then I tell her, in this really deep voice, 'Why Mother, I feel more manly already.'"

"Don't laugh," Teddy warns me, "you'll jiggle the needle. I'm almost done."

I still myself, and he tells me there's a little reward waiting for me when this is over.

"'Honestly, Teddy,' she says, sitting beside me on the edge of the bed. 'I had no intention of upsetting you with my little gift. I simply thought these sheets would be more—you know—*bachelory*.'"

Eyes still closed, I picture Teddy's mother sagging in defeat. "Sounds to me like she wants to be part of your private life. Misguided, but nice."

"I suppose," says Teddy. "One thing though, my mother hasn't sat on the edge of my bed since the times I stayed home from school with the flu."

There's a silence during which tiny dots flicker and swerve

on the underside of my eyelids, and I think of the chaos thriving in my blood: waggling bacteria, clustered cells, and maybe the thing I dread the most. *If I'm negative,* I tell myself, *I'm never going to have sex again.* It's a resolution I've made before. I'll be abstinent for a couple of months, until I'm too lonely to stand it anymore. I try to stay safe, I really do, but it's hard to guard against your own longing, not to mention depressing. I'm bound to slip, just a little, kissing despite a cut in my mouth or sucking cock without a condom. And I won't regret it. Until the next test.

Teddy says, "I remember eavesdropping on a game my parents used to play when they had friends over for drinks. Mom would ask everyone to think of a book or movie title, then add the phrase: 'between the sheets.'"

"Do one," I say.

Teddy thinks. "*Great Expectations Between the Sheets.* Now you," he says.

"*The Prince and the Pauper Between the Sheets.*"

"*The Color Purple Between the Sheets.*"

"*How Green Was My Valley Between the Sheets.*"

"*How to Be Your Own Best Friend Between the Sheets.*"

"*Eat Well and Live Better Between the Sheets.*"

I feel giddy, as though the two of us could do this forever. In the darkness I picture every kind of sheet, washed of sweat and semen and blood, flapping on an endless line. That you can put just about anything between them and make a kind of sense, or at least an interesting innuendo, suddenly seems miraculous, rich with possibility.

"You're done," says Teddy, and I open my eyes. The tourniquet comes loose with a snap. He presses a cotton ball where the skin has been punctured, and I hold it there till the bleeding stops. Teddy rolls his chair toward a little refrigerator and, when he opens the door, I notice vials of other patients' blood, fates lined up in a neat red row.

"Finally my mother gave in and told me to exchange them for the kind of sheets I want. 'Get a whole bouquet if it makes you happy.' When I put my arm around her she said it again, but the second time she really meant it." Teddy sets my sample in the rack, peels off his rubber gloves. He rummages inside the refrigerator and pulls out, of all things, a carton of orange juice, pouring some for me and some for himself. The picture on the side of the carton—an orange squeezed of one glistening drop—makes me realize how much blood I've given, how thirsty I am. Teddy swivels toward me. "Compliments of the clinic," he says, "and your resident phlebotomist."

Phlebotomist!

Together we raise our paper cups.

old birds

My father calls one afternoon to ask if I've made funeral arrangements. "For you," I ask, "or for me?"

"I know this is a morbid subject," he says, "but your number's gonna be up someday just like everybody else's. You could be walking down the street, minding your own business and—wham! Heart attack or truck, you'll never know what hit you. It wouldn't hurt to be prepared."

"I've already made plans," I tell him.

"So you couldn't use a casket?"

"I'm going to be cremated."

His hearing aid whines. "You're what?"

"I'm going to be cremated!" I shout. The phone is in the spare room I use as an office. Sketches are taped to my drafting board, blueprints spread across the floor.

"Your mother's sister, Estelle, was cremated," my father informs me. "You probably don't remember her because she died before you were born, but let me tell you her ashes were heavy, all those little bits of bone. Of course, Estelle was a big gal. Zaftig, we called it. Jake, her husband, invented the windshield wiper, but the idiot didn't apply for a patent and that's how he ruined their lives."

"I see," I said. The ringing phone had awakened me from an afternoon nap, but I was too embarrassed to tell my father. He likes to point out that, even though he's the senior citizen, I'm the sedentary man in the family, a family that consists of him and me. I often crawl into bed toward the end of the day and contemplate a project, and not even my inexhaustible father can convince me that lying there isn't work. Of course, to the naked eye it looks like I'm loafing, when buildings are actually taking shape—elevations, complex floor plans, isometric drawings instead of dreams. I once read that Albert Einstein spent hours lying in bed, his arm suspended over the edge of the mattress, a stone clasped in his hand; if he drifted off, his palm would open and the stone woke him when it hit the floor. It was here, in the ether of half-sleep, that he claimed to discover his finest ideas. Anyway, no matter how proud my father is of famous Jews, he'd be quick to remind me that I'm no Einstein, and that lying down in daylight is a waste of time.

Now that he's eighty-five, my father's hands shake and his thoughts are often muddled, but his energy never seems to wane. When she was alive, my mother used to say that my father plugged himself into a wall socket at night in order to recharge his battery—"a battery," she liked to joke, "that I haven't seen since our honeymoon." Despite a slew of infirmities and the medications keeping them in check, my father could be the subject of a longevity experiment, though he's been obsessed with his imminent death for the last ten years.

"I put a down payment on a casket today," he says. "Water-proof. Rosewood. Pretty as a piano. The funeral director—the son of a guy who hired me to carpet the place I don't know how many years ago—was having a two-for-one sale. That's why I'm asking; they're going cheap."

"Thanks," I say. "That's awfully . . . thoughtful."

"You should see how that shag held up. Still as white and fluffy as a cloud. The perfect pile for Haven of Rest."

Only then do I hear the whoosh of passing traffic. I brace myself. "Dad," I ask, "where are you?" Silence as my father no doubt peers around for a familiar landmark, squinting at street signs, cocking his head.

"You'd think someone would have the common decency to help me open a jar of peanut butter," he says. I'm certain he's holding the jar up to show me—it's Jif or Skippy, one of the brands my mother used to buy—as though I could see it, reach through the phone and twist off the lid. "I'm hungry!" he says.

My father wanders. And I don't just mean in conversation. The whole mess began after I'd moved him into an apartment complex in my neighborhood, one of the countless stucco boxes that line the streets of Hollywood, remnants from the building boom of the sixties. My father's apartment is on the second story, at the end of a narrow balcony whose wrought-iron railing vibrates with footfalls, like the string of some giant violin. Though modest by most standards, our old house had become too big for him in the decade since my mother's death, and only after he'd moved out did it occur to me that, instead of feeling lost in those rooms, my father might lose his way in the streets.

The first time it happened, I was driving home from a lecture called "Utopia: A Myth of Modernism?" when I stopped at a red light close to home and noticed an old man tottering up to the cars ahead of mine. He motioned people to roll down their windows, hoisting toward them what appeared to be a jar of pickles. Not until the man approached the car of the woman in front of me did I realize why he resembled my dad. I saw the woman quickly lock her doors and look away, as if my father were a derelict or specter. My first impulse was to punish her with a blast of my horn, but before I knew it, my father was standing beside my door. "Hey, Jimmy," he said with eerie nonchalance, handing me a jar of kosher dills. I stared at him, incredulous. "Arthritis," he remarked, as if that explained why he was standing in the middle of Franklin Avenue. It was a warm night. My windows were rolled down, the radio tuned to a local college station playing Japanese koto music, its warped chords, in the unexpected presence of my father, suddenly too lugubrious and loud. "Are they killing a cat?" he asked, nodding toward the radio. I clamped the jar between my knees and struggled with the lid, imagining an argument with the manager of the pickle factory, in which I gave him a tongue-lashing on behalf of all the arthritic people who'd had to do battle with his vacuum seals. Returning the open jar to my father, I inhaled a whiff of vinegar. I was about to insist that my father either get in the car or get out of the road, when the drivers behind me began to honk—I hadn't seen the light turn green— and my father shooed me off with a flap of his hand. In the rearview mirror, I saw him brave the glaring headlights and screeching brakes. Once he'd made it safely to the sidewalk, he sauntered toward the street where he lived, passing the windows of Dress for Less, Insta-Tan, and the House of Pies, those obstinate weeds of commerce sprouting all over town.

Only after I arrived home did I realize that pickle juice had sloshed onto my fly, and while dabbing my crotch with tap water, I tried to remember when I first became aware of having a father. I would have settled for any recollection, no matter how fleeting or incomplete: a vision of his hair, black and lacquered, or the cooing moon of his face floating above my crib. I had just turned fifty, and here I stood in the bathroom of a house I almost owned; the distance between me and my history seemed immense, unbridgeable. It was as if I'd never been an infant, or as if my father had always been old, aimless in his quest for favors, irate when the world refused to help.

"Listen to me, Dad," I say, gripping the receiver. "Ask the next person who walks by where you are." He could have been anywhere. Just last month he'd ended up in Norwalk, nearly twenty miles and two bus transfers away from the mailbox at his corner where, several hours before he phoned, he'd gone to mail a gas bill, sans the stamp.

"Where am I?" I hear him ask a passerby.

"What city?"

"No," barks my father. "What galaxy. Jimmy," he says in the general vicinity of the mouthpiece, "is it me, or are people plain stupid these days?"

"Screw you, old man."

"Dad . . ."

"Don't 'Dad' me. Here comes someone else."

"Hello?" It's the voice of a girl, maybe twelve, to whom my father must have handed the phone.

"Could you please tell me what street you're on and then give the telephone back to my father?"

"Is this a trick?" she asks. I can tell from her voice that she's smiling.

"My father's lost and you'd be doing me a big favor if you could look around for a street sign and let me know where he's calling from."

"Can't he see for himself?"

"Not very well."

"Is that why his glasses are so thick? They make his eyes look really creepy."

"What are you?" I hear my father ask her. "A goddamn optometrist?" Suddenly there's an airy swishing, and I picture the receiver swinging back and forth at the end of its cord, the booth abandoned.

"Hello?" I shout. "Hello?"

"You know," says my father, barely able to contain his rage. "You don't have to treat me like an invalid. I'm not some invalid!"

"I know," I say. "You're the opposite, whatever that is." I start to worry that I couldn't find him even if I organized a dragnet or called out the hounds. "Did that girl tell you where you are?"

"I'm on Central."

"Avenue?"

"She didn't say."

There are at least a dozen streets in Los Angeles named Central. From an urban-planning standpoint, this defeats the very idea of the plaza, the city square, the convergence of far-flung neighborhoods into a single place. Naming more than one street Central is like calling all of your children Fred.

"Does it look like downtown, Dad? Are there tall buildings around you?"

"Whaddya call tall?"

His question seems as a cryptic as a riddle. "Ten stories or more."

"I suppose you could call them . . . I see . . . oy," he sighs. "I'm too hungry to concentrate."

"Dad, if you're on Central Avenue downtown, I can be there in ten minutes, so don't worry."

"Who's worried?" he says, irritably. "I've got food, don't I?"

When he's deprived of protein, his blood sugar plummets, and confusion spins him like a wobbly top. Recently, I brought him Chinese takeout, and he was so hungry by the time he opened the door that he momentarily mistook me for his own reflection in a full-length mirror. A doctor would probably see this as proof of his mental deterioration. It also proved to me, however, that the older I get, the more alike we look: receding hairline, cleft chin, a tendency to freckle—hurtling toward the common end with which my father is so obsessed. "Maybe if you bang the lid of the jar against something, you can loosen it enough to open it by yourself. A little food might tide you over till I can get there."

After the impact, a deafening clatter. "Dad?"

"Incredible," he says. "The table for the phone book must have been stuck on with Scotch tape!"

"Are you okay?"

"How can you ask me that when I can't open the peanut butter! I paid good money for it! I'm ridiculous, Jimmy. What will I have to say for myself when I meet my maker?"

"You built a terrific business."

"Carpets?"

"How about me?" I say. "I must be a wonderful consolation for the indignities of old age." I laugh, alone.

"Were you sleeping when I called?"

"No, Dad. I was working."

"In bed, I bet."

"I'm working on a project for mid-Wilshire, near where your store used to be. It'll be low-income housing for the people who used to live in the neighborhood but can't afford to retire there."

"Bunch of old birds," he grumbles. "Half my friends are dead."

"Mine, too," I tell him.

He clears his throat. "You don't have the AIDS, though, do you, Jim?"

"No, but . . ."

"But what?" he says, alarmed.

But there was Greg, I want to tell him, *and Douglas and Jesse and Hank and Luis.* I try to remember each of my friends and, more precisely, the parts of themselves they fought to keep: their balance and vision and appetite, sensation in their fingers, control of their bowels. Yet some days all I recall of each man is how he let go of his body at last. No wonder cenotaphs and tombs make up the bulk of visionary architecture, with domes like eyes gazing toward heaven and endless flights of memorial steps: the dead have always outnumbered the living.

"I'm as healthy as a horse," I assure him.

"You and me both. But who knows for how long. When can you get me?"

"I've got an idea. Look on the telephone and tell me the number and area code."

"Someone must've scratched it out."

"What about the phone next to yours? Are you at a row of booths?"

"I wouldn't call them booths, exactly. They're like hoods on poles, with telephones inside."

A woman's prerecorded voice breaks in. "Please deposit fifty cents." Her inflections are all wrong, like a kitchen appliance trying to sound feminine.

My father says, "Fifty cents!"

"Take it easy," I tell him.

The woman repeats her request.

"I don't have any more change," shouts my father, "can't you wait till I get home and find my wallet?" It's hard to tell whether the plea is directed at me or the disembodied voice. "I thought I'd only be gone a minute. I'm in my slippers!"

"Dad," I say, trying to sound calm, "look in the booth next to yours and tell me the number; I'll call you back on *that* phone."

I wait. I pace. Phone pressed against my ear, I listen to muffled rush-hour horns. Eager as I am to find my father, I'm ready to crawl into bed again. I love the surrender, the stillness of repose, gravity like a stone I hold and won't let fall. It's almost dusk, but the light is warm for a California winter, when the sun shines obliquely and shadows are long. The house creaks as it does every evening, wind rustling the trees in my yard. *Old birds*, I keep thinking. And then it hits me: a retirement home that's an aviary! It's a weird idea, but workable. I can see the spacious atrium that houses flocks of exotic birds. Beneath a great skylight grow tropical palms and stands of banyan. The residents will gaze from their windows at airborne canaries, parrots engaged in extravagant disputes, finches preening and singing to their kind.

Then the telephone goes dead. Not dead, but that vast, desolate hiss of static, and I call out for my father one more time.

Seated at a long table, the members of the planning commission shuffle through papers and fiddle with their pens. They listen halfheartedly as I point to a drawing propped on an easel and describe how each of the seniors' rooms will overlook an aviary. "Pets have a beneficial effect on the mood and constitution of the elderly," I say, citing a recent study in *The American Journal of Geriatrics*. "Birds are especially inspiring to the aged due to their independence." There are coughs and whispers from the audience, which consists of people from the mid-Wilshire neighborhood and kooks who have nothing better to do than clog the chambers of city hall. Before I can finish, a woman with deep-set eyes and disheveled hair jumps up from the crowd and insists that the birds will spread fleas and other "vermin" to her cat, Langston, whose health, she tells us in a quaking voice, has been pitiful since kittenhood. Preposterous as her worry seems, the planning commission turns to face me, waiting for an answer.

Leon Hernandez is the ace up my sleeve. I gesture him forward from the first row and explain that he's the owner of the Asphalt Jungle, one of the oldest retailers of exotic birds in Los Angeles. "Mr. Hernandez has a degree in ornithology from California Polytechnic," I announce, leaning toward the microphone. This fact is followed by a reverent hush. Leon had been recommended to me by a fellow architect whose hotel pond is home to half a dozen swans, elegant and aloof when they aren't too busy hissing at the guests. So far I've only talked to Leon on the phone (we met for the first time earlier today) and as he walks toward me, I notice that he moves with the ease of certain middle-aged men; Leon simply fits inside his skin, uses his body to go about his business. The cat owner grows calm at the sight of him, nodding mechanically as he explains that birds don't carry fleas. "Macaws and cockatiels," he assures her, "are known for their meticulous grooming."

I thank Leon and finish my presentation. The council members caucus, finally approving the plans. Afterward, Leon and I meet in the lobby, where we continue our ongoing conversation about the bird population best suited to the aviary—finches, conures, plum-headed budgies—standing closer than is strictly necessary when discussing birds. Leon laughs and shakes his head. "Hell of an idea," he says. "How'd you come up with it?"

"It's too complicated to go into right now," I tell him, "but I have to share the credit with my father."

"Your father's interested in retirement homes, too?"

I picture my father wandering the streets. "Not yet," I say.

Half an hour later, driving up Western, I recall with almost supernatural clarity the forest of Leon's graying goatee, and his breath, minty from a stick of gum, as he uses words like "plumage," "tarsus," "contour feathers."

By the time I arrive home and push the button on my answering machine, I'm thinking up pretexts for another meeting with Leon. To want a man feels langorous, like waking up from a long nap, sensation slowly reclaiming my limbs. So many of my old lovers have died, and so many single men are symptomatic, that grief and desire have come to seem the same. Twenty years ago, I never would have believed that attraction could be fraught with loss, or that life could hold so many deaths without bursting at the seams.

There's a message from my father, who shouts into the mouthpiece as though I were the one who's hard of hearing. "I'm down at the House of Pies," he says. "I'll wait till you get here." We'd agreed to meet there for dinner at six-thirty. It's three o'clock now, and according to the answering machine, he left the message at a little after two. All of which means that he will have been waiting for over four hours by the time I arrive. I listen closely to make sure he understands that we're supposed to meet for dinner, not lunch, and sure enough he says, "If you're awake, Jimmy, pick up. I hope you remember we're having dinner tonight." Muzak burbles faintly in the background. "I'm hungry!" he says before he hangs up.

I toss the blueprints onto the studio floor. Without changing my clothes or washing my face, I hop back into the car and head down the hill to the House of Pies. With its four flared walls and steeply pitched roof, the building looks like a flash card of Home. Even from the parking lot I can see, through wide glass doors, the small waiting area with its hot-pink banquettes. My father sits, hands in his lap, staring into the middle distance with contented resignation. A few other elderly people are seated nearby, their faces dreamy, lax, abstracted, their heads of white hair as fine as mist. I turn off the engine and set the parking brake, overcome with an eerie feeling that, with its population of patient old folk, the waiting room at the House of Pies is the anteroom to heaven. It's so unusual to find my father in a state of rest that I sit for a minute and watch him not move.

"What's the matter?" he asks when I hurry inside. Only then do I feel exasperation tensing my face.

"It's only three-thirty," I say, checking the clock on the wall. The whole place smells of confectioner's sugar; I expect to see motes of it whirling in the air, drifts of it on the tabletops.

My father turns to check the clock, too. "So?" he says.

"I just didn't want you to wait forever."

Dad grabs the elbow of the hostess as she strolls past, clutching a stack of menus to her chest. "Have I been waiting forever?" he asks.

"I'm terribly sorry," she says, misunderstanding the point he's trying to make. "I'll seat you right away." She spins on her heel and, obedient lifelong patrons that we are, my father and I follow her into the main room. The place is almost empty in the lull between meals. Here and there, people are hunkered over wedges of pie. The hostess seats us at a corner booth and hands us each a menu. When she steps aside, I'm stunned to see Leon Hernandez sitting alone at a table across the room. He looks up from his plate and blushes, nodding hello. In the unguarded instant before he saw me, I sensed his familiar solitude and realized that Leon, roughly my age, must have lost a multitude to AIDS.

"A colleague?" asks my father. Before I can answer, he waves Leon over to our table. Leon points at himself. "Yeah, you!" shouts my father. A few happy pie-eaters lift their heads to look.

Leon approaches with a cup of coffee in one hand, a plate in the other. "Key lime is my weakness," says Leon.

"Amazing," I say, meaning the green, gelatinous pie, and meeting him here of all unlikely places. I scoot toward the wall, making room, and the man with whom I find myself smitten joins us for lunch-slash-dinner-slash-dessert.

"Dad, Leon Hernandez. Leon, Dad."

My father forgoes a hello. "Could you explain to me what my son actually does for a living?"

Here we go, I say to myself. "My father believes I'm a professional sleeper."

"A dreamer, maybe," says Leon.

Gratitude clangs inside my chest. "Leon and I were at city hall today, Dad."

My father looks at me skeptically.

I lift my tie and wave it in the air, offering proof.

"For Christ's sake," says my father. "Anyone can wear a tie. Just because I'm listed in the phone book doesn't make me . . . what's his name, that guy who invented the telephone? Alexander Graham Bell."

A moment of silence as the comment settles.

"Anyway," Leon continues, a little uncertainly, "James tells me the aviary was partly your idea."

My father has no idea what Leon is talking about, but he stays quiet and takes the credit.

"Leon here is an expert on birds, Dad."

"An expert?" says my father. "What's to know? They fly in the air and shit on your windshield."

On the outside, I'm smiling; on the inside, I'm crawling on my hands and knees, groping for composure. The heat of Leon's thigh next to mine, the spicy tang of his aftershave— my father's presence only increases the taboo factor, which in turn makes Leon more attractive, which makes acting normal more of a chore.

The waitress's arrival is a deus ex machina if ever there was one. My dad and I order entrees, Leon a refill of decaf. Once the waitress has gone, my father makes his paper napkin into a bib and tucks it into the collar of his shirt. He tells Leon he's eighty-five years old, then waits for the requisite admiration.

"I'm forty-eight," says Leon.

"Barely out of diapers," says Dad.

Leon sips his coffee. "You look remarkably fit for a man your age."

"I'm glad you think so, Leon." Here my father uses the melancholy inflection he's perfected over the years, a tone that suggests there are stories to be told; it's an invitation to probe beneath the surface, to touch the molten core of his woe;

there's arthritis, of course, and a miserable pittance from Social Security, not to mention the sadness of a man who believes he's come to the end of the road. "Looks," adds my father, "can be deceiving."

Leon doesn't take the bait.

"What my father is trying to say, Leon, is that we are dogged by the Grim Reaper every second of our lives. You never know when a blood clot or a mad gunman or runaway truck might make a slice of pie your last."

Leon stops eating.

My father glares at me. "Some people," he tells Leon, "fail to appreciate the . . . the . . ."

"The hardships of longevity? But I do, Dad. I really do." And at that moment—watching Leon squirm in his seat, anger dawning on my father's face—I feel older than Stonehenge. Beyond the windows, streets bluster with traffic and people, dull June sunlight burning through the clouds.

Leon says, "I should probably be going," and makes a move to rise.

"Sit," says my father. "My son could use the company. If you two will excuse me, I'm going to the little boys' room." He hoists himself up, lets out a grunt and shuffles away, the paper napkin flapping at his throat.

"Little boys' room," I say to Leon.

"Eighty-five, huh?"

"Born in 'nineteen aught nine,' as he says."

"'Aught,'" Leon echoes. "My grandmother says that."

"We make quite a couple, don't we?"

Leon raises his eyebrows.

"Me and my father."

After an interminable pause, talk turns to the Asphalt Jungle and Leon's pet, a parrot named Ike. "Parrots usually outlive their owners, so you have to be really committed. I won't sell an Amazon or an African gray to just anybody. I tell a prospective owner that they'll probably have to make a provision for the bird in their will; that tends to weed out the less dedicated people. Besides, it takes a certain type of person to live with an animal who answers back. I mean, it's easy to believe that dogs and cats are saying or thinking whatever you want. But when your pet says 'Shut up!' or whispers that you're pretty, it doesn't leave room for interpretation. Birds can be blunt."

"Ike's no fool," I say. Meaning that Leon *is* pretty, but he appears not to grasp the flattery, oblique as it is and channeled through a pet.

The waitress slaps down our plates and fills Leon's cup. "You want me to keep the liver and onions warm till the old guy gets back?"

"No, thanks," I say. "He'll be back any minute."

But several minutes go by and he doesn't return. I start to worry, and not only about my father, but about what the group of people being escorted to a nearby table are thinking when they see two men sitting together on the same side of a booth. I find myself hoping they'll notice the slab of liver at the third place setting, and at the same time I'm scolding myself for giving a damn what anyone thinks. I've always noticed when heterosexual couples sit side by side in restaurants and, as I suspected, it's completely unnatural; one has to crane around uncomfortably just to focus on a cheek or an ear. Leon is telling me about the time Ike made an unidentifiable noise, a muffled thrumming that turned out to be the sound of Leon's legs brushing together in a pair of wide-wale corduroy pants, and also about how Ike lets loose with a belch whenever he hears

Leon pour a carbonated drink. But I can barely listen; I'm off on a silent harangue about how teenage boys sometimes leave an empty seat between them at the movies because they're worried that sitting too close together will cast doubts on their manhood, and then I realize this is exactly what *I'm* worried about, except that I'm old enough to know better. A listless rendition of some Rolling Stones song tinkles through speakers recessed in the ceiling, and I can't for the life of me think of the title, either because the song has been made so bland as to be unrecognizable, or because age has played havoc with my memory. This onslaught of self-consciousness is just another reason to excuse myself and check the men's room.

Leon gets up to let me out. For a split second we stand face to face and I'm certain, or as certain as a fretful man can be, that he'd kiss me if the circumstances were different. This makes leaving him strangely momentous. As I walk toward the restrooms I turn to look back, and there he is, reclining in the vinyl booth, contentedly digesting pie and drifting into the distance.

I hurry down a long hall, past a pay phone and a drinking fountain. The men's room is small but immaculate, and when I call out, my voice bounces off tile walls, the emptiness confirmed by echoes. "Great," I say aloud, then catch my startled reflection in a mirror, thinking I've found him.

Back in the hall, it becomes clear that the only possible escape route is through the door at the far end. I follow my hunch, pushing hard on the safety bar. The door flies open to a narrow alley. Spilling from a Dumpster are mounds of brown fruit, moldering dough, and glinting pie tins. The second I step outside, I flinch from a shrill ringing and realize I've set off the fire alarm by opening the back door. Chefs and waitresses and busboys begin filing out of the building. Accustomed to false alarms, they gather in a sociable clump, lighting cigarettes, stretching and yawning, fishing in their pockets to weigh the day's tips. Next come the hostess and a man who, judging from the pie embroidered on his blazer, must be the manager. Together they help evacuate a group of grudging customers, one or two still chewing their food. No one is pleased by the Dumpster's rotting contents, the evening air alive with flies. Leon is last. "There you are," he says. "I was beginning to think you'd stuck me with the bill."

I tell him my father is gone, and explain how these disappearances have become more and more frequent during the past year. If I wasn't in such a hurry to find him, I'd also tell Leon that it seems as if my father has been trying to flee retired life, or evade his fate. When he first began to wander, Dad would pass by our old house, or peer into the window of his former store (it's now an upscale "eatery")—sad but understandable excursions. Yet he quickly lost his taste for nostalgia and set out for places even he couldn't predict; there were jars to be opened, bills to mail, countless destinations to forget. Anyway, I figure these things will someday get told if and when I come to know Leon, who offers to cover one end of the alley. We take off in opposite directions, looking into abandoned boxes and checking between parked cars. But nowhere is there a trace of my father, and we meet back where we started.

The manager has gone inside the restaurant to make sure there is, in fact, no fire. He shuts off the alarm, permits us to return. While everyone crowds their way back into the building and down the hall, the door to the ladies' room swings open and my father shuffles out, as surprised to be met by the customers and staff as they are to encounter an old man coming out of the ladies' room. His hearing aid, no doubt set off by the fire alarm, crackles with static. "There was no soap in the men's room," he blurts, "so I went in the women's. Is that some kind of crime?" Everyone stares. "Jimmy," he says, "you should get your friends at city hall to do something; we're living in a god-damn police state."

"The fire alarm went off, Dad."

"What?" He tinkers with his hearing aid.

"Carla," the manager says to the hostess, "could you please show these gentlemen back to their table."

"It's my fault," I explain. "I was looking for my father and I opened the rear door."

"What are you saying?" shouts my father. He plucks out the Bell-Tone and eyes it with contempt, small and beige in the palm of his hand. "Useless," he says.

I clasp my father's arm and urge him forward. "Where are you taking me?" he asks. Leon says, "It's okay, Mr. Markowitz." Dad's face is flushed, his breathing heavy. He looks at Leon as if he can't quite place this stranger. He glances at the waitresses and chefs, weary people summoned back to work. "I don't un-derstand what's happening!" My father wrenches himself from my grip, the hearing aid still whistling in his fist. He refuses to move until he understands, yet he won't be able to hear a word I say. And what would I tell him, anyway? That one blunder follows another? That all of us are lost? He cups his ear, cranes his neck, squints at me expectantly, and the paper napkin, light as a feather, slips from his collar and floats to the ground.

Ike waddles toward me across the wooden floor, up to no good. The closer he comes, the less trouble I have believing the the-ory that birds evolved from dinosaurs. I don't care how light his feathers, how hollow his bones: those eyes are little beads of malice, his claws like the tines of horrible forks. Ike took a disliking to me the very first time I came to visit Leon; I'd cooed to Ike as if he were a baby, holding out my finger and inviting him to perch. "Look at you!" he'd shrieked. Then he took a vicious bite, breaking the skin. Now a year has gone by and Leon says Ike's continued resistance is typical of an older bird (Ike is 15) whose instinct is to protect his mate (that would be Leon) from other birds, such as myself. Leon is in the bathroom getting ready to leave, and I wait for him on the couch, free to glower to my heart's content. Ike is undaunted. From his point of view I'm plucked and wingless, an easy mark. He stops at my feet and bobs his head, aiming one eye at a time toward my shoes. Before I know it, he chomps on a lace, which he swiftly unties by flapping backward. I clap my hands a couple of times but can't quite recall if this is how Leon disciplines Ike or applauds his antics. As I bend down to retie the shoe, Ike scuttles away, tail feathers twitching. Once he reaches safety he turns to face me, erupting with remembered banter. It doesn't take me long to realize he's imitating an exchange between Leon and his lover, Albert, who died five years ago. The bird takes both parts, changing pitch as he mimics two men calling to each other from what must have been opposite ends of the apartment: "Honey!" "What?" "Honey!" "What?" Ike's interpretation tends to emphasize the plaintive tone in their voices. It's as if he's trying to remind me that pair bonding, as the ornithologists call it, is a long and urgent conversation, like cries rising from a canopy of trees.

The one and only time Ike did an imitation of me was after I'd been on the phone with my father. I'd just moved Dad into a managed-care facility not far from where the retirement

home was being built. He'd begun to lapse into anxious silences, and after administering a battery of tests, a gerontolo-
gist diagnosed him with Alzheimer's; the impromptu trips and
unstamped letters may have been the earliest signs. After the
diagnosis, the names of places and people and things began to
elude him more and more. At a loss for words, my father found
it hard to complain, and complaint, after all, had been the
man's most eloquent assertion, proof of his superior sense in a
crazy world. Deafness only compounded the problem; when
he couldn't hear the words he'd forgotten, they faded irretriev-
ably and fast. Eventually, he lost the will to wander. Gripping
the arms of his BarcaLounger, he stayed put in it for hours on
end. Those proved to be difficult days in general. Construction
on the retirement home was over budget, and the company
fabricating the central skylights was being sued by a contractor
who claimed they leaked in the rain. All these delays meant
that the Asphalt Jungle was crowded with birds who were
slated to live in the atrium, and my clients had to pay for their
keep. According to Leon, nothing is worse than an idle bird,
and squalls of collective restlessness rang throughout the shop.
Anyway, after I hung up from talking to my father, Ike began
to scream in my voice: "How are you feeling? Is the food any
good? Do you like your room?" The sheer volume, the naked
impatience, made me ashamed. But worse were the parrot's
lengthy pauses, which stood for my father's side of things.

Leon emerges from the bathroom, wet hair combed back.
He bends down, touches his index finger to Ike's plump chest,
and lifts the bird from the floor. At the entrance to his cage, Ike
clings to Leon's finger and peers disdainfully at his avian play-
ground, with its bell, mirror, ladder and trapeze. Leon murmurs, "Hasta la vista!" But Ike perches firm.

"We have a very stubborn bird on our hands," says Leon, casting me a glance.

"Do we," I say.

Leon waggles his finger, which Ike rides like a rodeo cowboy, eventually screeching, "Cut that out!" The bird extends his wings just enough to make it impossible for Leon to slip him through the cage door. On the next attempt, Ike grips the bars with his beak and won't let go. Under normal circumstances, he would probably be left behind to fly around the apartment, shredding the magazines on the coffee table and plucking threads from the rug. But Leon decides we should take Ike with us to visit my father. "We'll be like those people who bring dogs into hospitals for the patients to pet," he says, brightening at the idea that parrots can be Good Samaritans. "I bet your dad will love it, Jimmy."

And Dad does. For a while, at least.

When Leon and I arrive, he's sitting in a chair, fully dressed yet sound asleep, his mouth hanging open. Each time I visit, the room strikes me as a little shabbier than I'd remembered, with its beige walls and dented pine dresser, the only piece of furniture to survive his former life. The air is ripe with the smell of disinfectant. Stuck here and there are the Post-It Notes I've left to remind him to soak his dentures every night and turn off the heater before he leaves.

Dad stiffens and opens his eyes when the door clicks shut behind us, trying to act as if he'd been awake. He still sees himself as a busy man, though his main occupation is to cling to this belief. Years ago, when I was a boy, I traveled with him to Whittier, Norwalk, and Pacific Palisades, which seemed to me then like neighboring states. He'd look at the floor appraisingly, then turn the pages of his sample book while discussing the virtues of hi-lo versus plush. There wasn't a room my father couldn't improve. Except this one, I think, glancing around.

"Mr. Markowitz," says Leon.

"Hello," says my father. "Pleased to meet you."

My father has met Leon a half a dozen times since their first encounter at the House of Pies. He never remembers who Leon is, but neither does he seem surprised to see him. Leon fits in the present tense, with its shifting population of strangers. Besides, Dad observes us standing close together and seems to understand that I'm fond of the man. He once asked Leon if I was his son. And Dad seemed pleased, or at least relieved, when Leon said yes.

I sit on the bed my father manages to make every day with a nurse's help. Leon takes a chair opposite my father, sets the carrying case on his lap, and unzips the lid. Up pops a quizzical, feathered head. Ike looks around and opens his mouth, exposing the small black bud of his tongue. Dad's eyes widen. His lips press together, forming a "B."

"That's right!" I shout. "It's a bird, Dad. Leon's bird. His name is Ike. We've brought him to visit you."

"How do you like your room?" screams Ike. "Is the food any good?"

My father gasps in disbelief, stares at this brazen, garrulous parrot.

Leon turns to look at me with what can only be described as parental pride.

"I hate to burst your bubble," I say, "but he's heard me talking with my father on the phone."

"I *know* he didn't come up with the phrases himself," counters Leon. "But he used the words in *context*."

"He . . . he . . . ?"

"Yes, Dad. He's a parrot. He talks."

And suddenly I know what triggered Ike to recall the conversation with my father. Then, as now, my voice is loud and overeager; I refuse to give up the shouting match that has kept us engaged for forty-odd years, two men trying to have the last word.

In his excitement, my father suddenly lunges. Ike, of course, doesn't have time to distinguish between glee and aggression. Feathers rise on the nape of his neck. Before Leon can tighten his grip, the bird screeches and flaps toward the ceiling, clouds of dander sloughed from his wings.

My father dashes across the room and raises the window. Leon doesn't see me leap from the bed and struggle to shut it; he's jumping toward the ceiling, snatching at the bird and making the kissing noises that usually get his attention. Ike, however, spots me through an eye on the side of his head. He takes a dive, smashing against the upper pane. With a dull thud, he falls to the floor. Leon dives too, landing on his stomach. I can hear the breath punched from his lungs. He skids a few feet across the polished linoleum and reaches out to trap the stunned bird. Dad just stands there. He doesn't understand what the fuss is about; we brought him a bird, and birds, as any idiot knows, belong in the air. I push as hard as I can, and all at once the window comes unstuck and crashes down, the glass shattering. Ike rallies at the deafening noise and lifts off the floor, sailing through the broken window. I try to catch him before he escapes, and feel his feathers brushing past my hands.

I manage to shout Leon's name, but he's run out the door and down the hall.

"Oh, no," says my father, noticing a drop of blood on the windowsill. I've cut my forearm, but neither of us moves. We watch Leon race down the front steps of the nursing home and into the busy street. For a while, Ike flies overhead, and Leon keeps pace directly beneath him, bellowing into the heavens every familiar phrase he can think of, every pet name, ridiculous endearment, anything to bring the bird back. His voice grows dimmer and yet more desperate the farther he runs. Several pedestrians step out of the way as Leon charges past. One or two shield their eyes against the sun and see the creature gliding eastward, a blur against the smoggy sky. Leon stops to catch his breath; even from here I can see him heaving, the back of his shirt drenched with sweat, his figure so small I could hold it in my palm. "It's in the big place," my father announces, referring to the bird. I wonder if I should scold him, insist he apologize when Leon returns. But what would scolding mean to a man whose history has come to this: One moment separate from every other. And then another. Dad turns from the window, sidesteps shards of broken glass. He settles in his chair and begins to forget. The bird keeps rising. And then he's gone.

Leon and I are seated behind a sheer white curtain, peering out as if from the afterlife at guests who gather in the small chapel. My father's rosewood coffin, the one he bought on a payment plan, is surrounded by sprays of white gladiolas and elevated in the center of the stage. Prerecorded music is piped through the ceiling, just as it is at the House of Pies, though these are the notes of a massive organ, somber, vibrato. I spot Jake, my aunt Estelle's husband, milling near the door; he's trim and in his early sixties, far too young to have invented the windshield wiper, and I wonder what possessed my father to tell me that story; had he made a mistake, believed it himself? This will be his legacy: hundreds of facts that don't add up, a life lived in degrees of confusion, but lived nonetheless.

A hush falls as Rabbi Weissman, new to my father's temple, walks up to the podium, clears his throat, and with all the drama and sanctity he has in him, eulogizes a man who bears almost no resemblance to my dad. Since he mentions my mother and the carpet store, I know he isn't describing someone else. Still, Leon and I look at each other when he lifts his arms majestically and says, "Everyone who came into contact with Abe Markowitz appreciated his easygoing nature. Abe was a man who never complained. A lover of life. A solver of disputes."

"Why not 'cantankerous'?" I whisper to Leon. "'Cantankerous' isn't so bad."

"Or 'impulsive,'" says Leon.

"'A man of the streets.'"

"'A liberator of imprisoned birds.'"

I take Leon's hand. The day Ike escaped, we'd waited in my father's room for the glazier to come. Leon stood by the window, spent from the chase and hoping that some fluke of avian behavior might compel the bird to return. The ornithologist in him knew better, however. As Leon himself once told me, parrots whose wings are never clipped grow up believing they own the air; they're like egotists flying wherever they please, so the chances that Ike would come back were slim. During his vigil, Leon reminisced about all the pithy phrases he'd taught the bird—My Latin name is *Psittacus erithacus Linnaeus!* What's yours?—and all the words Ike learned on his own. It was as if Leon had to go through the animal's entire vocabulary before he could begin to grasp his absence. That day at the nursing home, and for weeks afterward, I apologized repeatedly on my father's behalf, trying to express the regret he couldn't muster,

to find the words he couldn't recall. If I wasn't able to understand Leon's affection for Ike, this much was clear: I loved the
man for loving a bird. I nailed up posters with a photo of Ike,
promising a hefty reward. At one point I offered to buy Leon a
new parrot, canary, or parakeet. "They're called budgerigars,"
Leon said curtly, "not parakeets. Anyway, it's Ike that's gone. I
miss him in particular, and I'm going to miss him no matter
what you do."

The organ crescendos, and the rabbi asks the small group of
mourners to stand. Except for a few distant relatives and my father's former accountant, I don't recognize most of the people
filing past the coffin, which I'd asked the funeral director to
keep closed. My mother's casket had been open, and the sight
of her sallow, expressionless face has never left me. "Keep the
damn thing shut," I told the director. "I'm tired of crying at funerals. I'm tired of funerals, period. And while we're at it, I
wish—forgive me—you were out of business. Oh, I know," I
blurted, cutting him off, "death makes life precious and all that
crap, but I really don't care. I wish it didn't exist." The man
nodded officiously and made a note to keep the casket closed,
assuming, I suppose, that I was yet another client delirious
with grief.

The service seems even more unreal when we move outside.
In order to get to my father's plot, the funeral party has to walk
through a knoll of headstones, each chiseled with a span of
dates separated by a single dash, hardly a scratch in the marble.
The graveside proceedings take place in full sunlight, and there
are moments when I simply want to walk away, find a distant
patch of grass and bask in the sun, especially as the cantor's
lament drifts across the cemetery. Leon and I are seated in the
first row of folding chairs, facing the hole into which the cof-

fin will be lowered by a system of pulleys. The earthen walls are smooth and moist, and it occurs to me that graves are the inverse of architecture, a shelter hollowed out for the dead rather than raised for the living.

I'm startled from my reverie when the rabbi hands me a shovel. I hadn't been listening, but I remember from countless other funerals how the first shovelful of dirt is tossed onto the casket by someone close to the deceased, a loved one given the dubious honor of sealing the loss, once and for all. I stand up, stab the shovel into a mound of soil and fling it into the grave. Dirt hits the coffin's glossy lid. "Pretty as a piano," my father had said, and to make the moment bearable, I imagine the strings and hammers disappearing, the pedals and keys unreachable.

Later, back at my place, I tell Leon I need to lie down, and he says he could use a nap too. On the way to the bedroom, we pass my studio, where plans for a hotel in Santa Barbara are taped to the drafting board. Finally finished, the retirement home led to more commissions and an interview in *Progressive Architecture*. I made sure to tell the interviewer that the idea for the aviary came about when my father phoned me, stranded on Central without his wallet, but the anecdote didn't make it into print.

Exhausted from the service, from giving and receiving sympathy, Leon and I fall into bed. Although we like to spend time in our separate places, it's hard to fall asleep without him tossing and snoring and taking up room. Afternoon light filters through the curtains, turns crimson when I close my eyes. This nap is deeper, more fevered than most. I wander for what seems like hours through one of those improbable futuristic cities I loved as a boy. Buildings rise on slender poles, some of them hovering high in the air. Roads are enclosed in clear plastic tubes, parks and plazas covered by domes. Except, in the dream the buildings are empty, the plastic yellowed, the shapes of vehicles obsolete. Then comes a vague awareness that I'm flailing. Leon and I begin to stir, struggling against the weight of sleep. We work the moisture back into our mouths. We blink our eyes and reach for each other. After a dazed and difficult waking, there we are.